THE TROY LEGACY

First published in Great Britain in 2024 by
The Book Guild Ltd
Unit E2 Airfield Business Park,
Harrison Road, Market Harborough,
Leicestershire. LE16 7UL
Tel: 0116 2792299
www.bookguild.co.uk
Email: info@bookguild.co.uk
Twitter: @bookguild

Typeset in 11pt Minion Pro

Printed and bound by CPI Group (UK) Ltd, Croydon, CR0 4YY

ISBN 978 1835740 255

British Library Cataloguing in Publication Data.
A catalogue record for this book is available from the British Library.

THE TROY LEGACY

J RYAN

The Book Guild Ltd

ONE

THE RED SAIL

The sail slowly appearing on the horizon is the colour of a pale blood stain. Paros, our foreman, sees me pause my work and stare at it. The other men carry on; Sparta is short of ships with so many having gone to the war, and we are heavily time-pressured.

Paros's grey eyes take in the sail, and now the hull of a bireme. We're on a lee shore and the wind is sweeping them rapidly towards us. The figure of a broad-shouldered man stands at the prow, his cloak billowing with the following wind. Paros resumes his work, saying, 'That'll be King Odysseus of Ithaca.'

'What does he want with us?'

'It's you he wants, Damian. We'll be sorry to lose you, lad.'

'All this way for one soldier?'

And now the figure of a younger man appears behind

that of the king. The sun blazes on a shock of copper-coloured hair and rippling muscles; even from this distance it's clear that here is a formidable warrior. At a few hundred yards offshore, the oarsmen back-row to hold position. A powerful voice hails us. 'We are seeking Damian, son of Stergios the shipbuilder!'

I am already walking down the beach and into the waves, as Paros calls back, 'This is he, sir!' Knowing that I have to swim for it, as they will never get off this beach with the onshore wind, I throw myself into the water. I pride myself on being a strong swimmer, like all Spartans; in a few minutes, I am at the prow and pulling myself up the rope they throw to me. Odysseus is shouting orders to the oarsmen. He of the red hair motions me towards an unmanned oar and I set to the task. It is a tough one. With the sail now reefed, and two levels of oarsmen with thirty to port and the same to starboard on each deck, the eighty-foot-long ship is slowly turned into the waves, and we start to make way. And so begins my voyage to the mighty walls of Troy.

*

Poseidon represents a far worse threat than pirates in the seas around Greece. He has saved countless kingdoms from invasion by sinking hostile navies without trace. As we head through the Cyclades, howling squalls hit us one after the other. While the useless sail is still reefed, we battle to keep the ship heading straight into the waves, which reach ten feet at times. With my shipbuilder's instincts, I look approvingly at the stout construction of our craft. She cannot have been mouldering on the beaches of Troy for the last nine years; she looks quite recently built and well maintained.

One of my comrades-in-oars sees me appraising the oak beams of the hull, as we bend to our task in a regular rhythm. He grunts, 'You'd be right in thinking this ship is not from Troy. We commandeered her in Skyros when we picked up Redhead.'

'The mighty warrior with the red hair?'

My comrade's voice is quieter as he says, 'Don't get on the wrong side of him or he'll take your head off.'

Just as quietly, I ask, 'Who is he?'

'A killing machine, like his father. That is Pyrrhos, the son of Achilles.'

'Is he to take command of the Myrmidons now that his father is slain?'

My colleague hauls on his oar as a larger-than-usual wave showers us with spray. 'You Spartans are well informed.'

'We have an efficient spy network.' I save my breath for rowing after this exchange. But with a dull sense of inevitability, I wonder if I too am a replacement for a dead father.

*

Being a mariner in Sparta's navy as well as a shipbuilder, I know much of the Aegean well, although I have never sailed as far as Troy, Skyros being my limit. The Aegean, while it has no tides to speak of, is like a temperamental thoroughbred: hard to predict and very powerful. The prevailing Etesian winds blow from the north, and so would have given King Odysseus a fast voyage from Troy to Skyros to collect Pyrrhos, and from there to Sparta would also have been largely running before the wind with a full sail. Now that we are beating into the Etesians, it's a different story.

Usually, the wind starts in the early afternoon and dies out at sunset. However, there can be times when the wind perseveres at night and blows over many days – sometimes up to ten days. This results in the production of waves higher than ten feet and ceaseless hard work for the oarsmen; our eighty-foot craft can ride the waves only if she is kept with her prow-mounted ram pointing head-on at the surf. Without a deep keel – as these ships are designed to be beached not moored – she would roll straight over if we were turned sideways to the waves.

After many days and nights of rowing, with food a hastily snatched mouthful here and there and no sleep, the wind finally abates when we have drawn north of Skyros. We pull into a sheltered cove on a small eastern Aegean island, where the exhausted mariners can rest, drink and eat. The ship is beached and, flexing stiff limbs, we set to roasting flying fish, cramming bread into our bellies and drinking well-watered wine.

I am sitting in the sand with two of my fellow oarsmen, when they mumble an excuse about stretching their legs and amble off. Looking behind me, I see the reason for their departure. The powerful form of Pyrrhos is striding towards me, his shock of red hair still ragged and wet from the sea. I stand respectfully as he approaches, but he motions me to sit back down and seats himself cross-legged opposite. I offer him a large piece of fish on my knife; he seems surprised but takes it with a nod of thanks, accepting some bread too. He eats ravenously, as though he has had nothing at all for days, not even the morsels that we were able to grab between oar strokes. Looking at his dark eyes, thick brows and firm-set jaw, I sense that here is a boy who is only sixteen like me but who is so driven that he forgets to eat. Maybe to drink, too; I pass him the flask. He takes some gulps and gives it back to me with a tightening of the mouth that could pass for a smile. No words have been exchanged during these transactions, but I am not a naturally garrulous person (no Spartan is), so this suits me.

When we are called back to the ship to continue rowing through the advancing night, Pyrrhos strides quickly ahead of me. Once we have pushed off and turned to our northerly course, I am ordered to a different seat, near the stern and just in front of where King Odysseus himself sits in the command position. My fellow oarsman is now Pyrrhos. Once more, no words are exchanged because no word is necessary. We both prefer a companionable silence.

*

We are now on a north-easterly course to Troy, so the sail can be hoisted to catch some air on a beam reach. Occasionally, the wind veers and the sail snaps and quivers, but for the most part the new trajectory makes for less work. At one point, with dawn breaking across a lapis lazuli sea, the oarsmen are taking it in turns in alternate pairs to allow for some rest time. And it is during one of my breaks that

I am ordered up for an audience with King Odysseus, as he sits regally in the command seat at the stern of the ship. Without taking his eyes from the horizon, he says quietly, 'Do you know why you are going to Troy, Damian?'

'With respect, no, sir.'

'It is for a project so secret that death by crucifixion is the unconditional sentence for anyone who breathes a word of it.'

'Then I'd rather that you didn't tell me, sir.'

King Odysseus of Ithaca now turns to look at me. Something in his dark eyes tells me that I have given him the answer he wanted. I have heard much about this man's cleverness, his wily ways in the manipulation of men. He continues, 'You will have to know in due course, in order to carry out your work. What I can tell you now is that we want your shipbuilding skills first and foremost.'

'I will do my very best, sir.'

As I return to my position next to Pyrrhos and we both take up our oars again, he speaks for the first time. 'He could also have told you that your father has been killed.' The voice is deep for a teenager. Almost a growl, in fact. But there is pity for a fellow orphan in that growl.

I nod in acknowledgement. In my father they have lost, not just a valiant fighter and leader of men, but also a skilled shipbuilder. As soon as I could walk, he began teaching me all I know about boats. And though it is nine years since I last saw him, I can still remember the quietness of his voice and the strength of his arms and hands, as he made planks of oak bend and bow to build hulls and turned single young fir trees into fifteen-foot oars.

But now the question taps at my mind: are the Greeks refurbishing their ships and building new ones because they have given up on conquering Troy? I am sure that the answer resides in the head of the extremely clever king who commands our ship, and I am equally sure that it will not be in the affirmative, or am I asking the wrong question?

*

Positioned between the mouths of the Simois and Scamander rivers, the city of Troy is the capital of a highly prosperous state which controls the narrow straits of the Hellespont, the regions of the Thracian peninsula and a number of other districts and islands. I was seven years old when my father was called to follow our king Menelaus, whose wife Helen had been abducted by the Trojan prince Paris; that, after many days of generous hospitality provided to this traitor. And although the military initiative was to be led by the brother of Menelaus, the mighty King Agamemnon of Mycenae, supported by an army which had united most of the Greek world, my tutors expressed concern about the undertaking. They were in agreement that Troy was one of the largest cities in the Aegean and – with its control over a number of prosperous trade routes – one of the richest and most powerful. Not only that, but the Trojan army was known to be one of the strongest and certain to be more disciplined than the disparate troops from many different Greek kingdoms. Troy's royal family could also count on numerous loyal allies to rally to its support.

Old Demosthenes, my history tutor, felt that the severest aspect of the siege was always going to be the supply lines. 'The Greeks will have the worst of it; how are they going to feed their vast army? It's easy for the Trojans, with their control of the land and the trade routes. But Agamemnon will struggle to have food and drink shipped in with the Trojan navy on watch!'

My maths tutor, Nicias, who was half the age of the venerable Demosthenes, felt that the decider was always going to be the sheer strength of Troy's defences. 'They have withstood many sieges in the past and inflicted heavy losses on the invaders. They say that Troy is built so that it is impossible to get siege engines within range of the walls.'

Nine long and punishing years later, my tutors seemed to be right. We had heard that, due to supply problems, Agamemnon could never deploy the full force of his troops because of the numbers who had to be sent foraging off the land and surrounding settlements.

The most recent news, from a member of Sparta's elite youth secret service, the Krypteia, was even more disturbing. 'The tide seems to be turning against the Greek forces. They requested a temporary truce so that they could burn and bury the thousands of their dead. This was granted so that the Trojans could do the same. The Greeks created a mass grave for the bones, which they constructed as a bunker protecting their camp and their ships like a long wall. Then, to further defend the camp, they dug a trench in front of the burial mound so that the Trojan chariots could not cross.'

Demosthenes shook his grey head. 'You have to ask, is a woman – even one reputed to be the most beautiful in the world – really worth this loss of life?'

To which Nicias quickly responded, 'Menelaus might be doing this to get his wife back, but I think we all know that's not what motivates his brother Agamemnon. Troy has power and riches that he wants for himself, at any price!'

And what a terrible price, for both sides. Prince Hector cut down by Achilles and his remains dishonoured by being dragged through the dust round the walls of Troy by Achilles' chariot. Achilles himself humiliatingly slain by the coward Paris, the criminal who had begun the whole thing by rupturing the ancient laws of hospitality and stealing the wife of his host, along with much treasure. And thousands of heroes, unnamed and unsung, who went into the battle full of valour and whose bones were now piled in that burial mound behind the Greeks' last-ditch defence.

*

Evening is painting the western horizon with red-streaked clouds when the lookout sights land. Now all rowers are shipping their oars, and the sail is reefed in preparation for a controlled landing. As our ship approaches, we see first the hulls ranged for miles along the beach; I can guess that most by now will be falling victim to rot. Then we can make out the glow of campfires in between the Greek huts. Further in, and dim in the dusk, rises the high hill on which the walls and watchtowers of Troy are built. The huge city effortlessly dominates the straggling huts and beached ships of its attackers; my heart lurches as I survey the results of years of deathly struggle. And I cannot help tears stinging my eyes, as I finally realise that I will never see my father again. That his charred bones are mingled with the millions of others inside that bunker where, even in death, Greek soldiers bar the way to defend their living comrades.

Glancing briefly at my companion, I see that he is surveying the Troy shores as intently as I was just now. And, while his dead father's remains will have been laid to rest in his own private tomb, next to that of his beloved friend Patroclus, where fitting tribute can be paid, the faint glisten on his face tells me that Pyrrhos is grieving as I am, although I don't know if he has any memory of his famous father. Then there's a jolt as the ship touches sand, and everyone is jumping into the water to pull our stout bireme up onto the beach. As Pyrrhos disappears into the night to join his Myrmidons, I find myself being ordered into a marching column and setting off along the beach with just the stars to light our way.

My first colleague on the ship is marching with me. He says gruffly, 'Did Redhead shed any light on what you've been conscripted for?'

I shake my head. 'I only know that breathing a word brings death by crucifixion.'

He laughs. 'You'll know soon enough. But I can tell you that you're not here as a fighter.'

'And not here to repair ships so that the Greeks can cut and run?'

'No. But we're done with fighting to break Troy. It's indestructible by force.'

'I'd heard of its reputation.'

'It's well earned. This is no ordinary coastal citadel. It's a vast fortress city with *six* lines of defence.'

'The first being the Trojan army?'

My companion grimaces. 'Who outnumber us and fight like gods; now that we have lost Achilles, everything is going against us.'

'Then, presumably there is a defensive trench to keep out our chariots?'

'Which is also fiercely defended by Trojan troops. We've sent out night sorties to try to backfill and bridge it, but they work in never-ending shifts.'

'And if you did succeed in crossing the trench, you'd then be up against the walls of the lower city: the third line of defence.'

'We can't get the siege engines within range of those walls without bridging the trench. But even if we did, you've seen the size of the hill that Troy is built on. Every row of houses is in a higher position than the preceding one. Their roofs are the perfect base for Trojan archers, slingers and javeliners, while the ground floors are protected by heavily armoured troops. Their fourth line of defence goes on and up forever!'

'And it's numbers again, isn't it? They've had allies pouring to their aid for years.'

'And they'd use women and children to put out the fires if necessary.'

I hazard a guess. 'So the fifth line of defence must be the outer wall of the citadel?'

My companion nods. 'Five metres thick and eight

metres high. Fully rounded without a corner anywhere that a siege engine could make a dent in.'

'Hard to imagine how any siege engine could operate on those slopes.'

'Exactly! And there's still the inner wall of the citadel before you're anywhere near the palace.' My companion exhales heavily. 'It's a wonder we carried on so doggedly for so long, when any fool could see we were wasting our time as well as all those lives.'

We've reached a cave set into the cliff, heavily guarded; within is the glow of torchlight. Our column halts and stands to attention, as a giant emerges from the cave and surveys what the sea has brought in. He would tower above Pyrrhos, with massive thighs and bull-like shoulders from which rises a thick bull neck. My colleague whispers, 'Epeios of Phocis, the pugilist. At the funeral games of Patroclus, he beat Euryalus to a pulp. At the funeral games for Achilles he fought Acamas, son of Theseus, to a stalemate.'

Mesmerised, I watch as the giant paces slowly along our lines. He has slits for eyes, deep set into a face that looks carved from stone. He says, in a surprisingly quiet voice that can barely be heard over the distant lapping of waves, 'If any man does not know the penalty for talking about this, let him raise his hand.'

No one moves. The giant nods to a lieutenant. 'Give them saws and take them to their tasks.'

The rest of that night is spent sawing down oak trees and carrying the wood into the cave to add to the piles already there. Then, as dawn trails a dull fire across the horizon, we are formed into a column for the march back to camp, extremely hopeful that there will be food and drink to revive our flagging bodies. Just as the column is about to move off, while the next shift is arriving, the giant's lieutenant motions me to follow him back into the cave. Epeios is sitting on a boulder, watching the new arrivals collect their saws. I stand before him respectfully, well aware of the strength in those massive fists.

He says in his low voice, 'You are Damian, son of Stergios the shipbuilder?'

'Yes, sir.'

'For how long have you been building ships?'

'I started my training aged two, sir, so fourteen years.'

'And would you consider yourself a master of your craft, son of Stergios?'

'I am always trying to do things that bit better, sir.'

He pauses before asking me, 'How good do you think you would be at building a wooden horse that can hold thirty men?'

*

I never did return to the camp after that meeting. My thoughts in turmoil, but with ideas bubbling and boiling, I took a stick and began to draw in the sand. The heart of the design was an upturned hull which would form the back of the horse; the ship's ribbing would be the ribs of the horse. The length would be that of a ship which could accommodate thirty crew facing each other, fifteen to a side. Rushing here and there like a madman, I drew to size, not to scale, so that Epeios would have as clear an idea as possible of what I was proposing. A further, shallower hull would form the underside, with a concealed trap door to allow for exit. The height of the horse would be such that a rope ladder would be provided to allow the men safely to descend. The legs and tail would be constructed in the way we build masts, capable of sustaining the massive weight of the horse's abdomen, neck and head and the men within it.

Then there was the question of transportation. 'Where will you wish the horse to be taken to, sir?'

But it's not Epeios who answers. King Odysseus has approached completely silently while I am dashing around, sketching and explaining in a fever of excitement. Epeios has seen him, but I spin round in surprise. 'It will be left just outside the entrance to our camp, with a thank offering to Athena for our safe return home. The camp itself will have been burned and the army sailed to the island of Tenedos to await the signal. Now, what are your plans for transporting the horse to the camp?'

'We will need two wooden masts as the wheelbase beneath a sled to which the horse will have been secured, sir. They will need to be as wide a diameter as we can make them.'

'Excellent!' King Odysseus turns to his colleague, who completely dwarfs the pair of us. 'I think we owe this young inventor some good meat and wine, don't you, my friend? His stomach must by now be cleaving to his spine.'

His words are the most welcome I have heard in a long time. Towards the back of the cave, a whole pig is roasting on a spit, and housekeepers are bustling around with bread and flagons of wine. I smelt the cooking odours when we first set off with our saws into the forest, and my mouth watered. And so, I sit down with the wily king and the soft-voiced giant and feast to my heart's content. And I am now to live here as the overseer of the horse, until this creature of King Odysseus's imagination is built and ready to penetrate the unassailable walls of Troy.

It is an audacious plan, one that could only have come from this warrior and statesman renowned for his cunning. To the Trojans, the horse is a sacred animal. When they see the Greek camp burned and their ships gone, with a votive offering to Athena all that remains, you can picture their wild relief at this awful war being over. But will they actually fall entirely for the deceit and take the horse into the heart of Troy? King Odysseus must know that this is a gamble where he is throwing his last dice. He must have had to employ all his genius to persuade Agamemnon to accept his plan.

While the sawing-down of oak trees continues by daylight and torchlight, I am allowed to catch a few hours' sleep, which by then I desperately need. With a full stomach and heavy eyes, on a comfortable bed of animal skins, I plunge straight into oblivion.

*

With the intensity of the shifts bringing in oak wood from sunrise to sunrise, it isn't long before I estimate that we have enough for our horse. Now it has to be cut into the different lengths and thicknesses required, and it has to be bent to make the many curving contours that you see in a ship's hull. There are different ways of getting wood to bend – some by direct application of fire, others by boiling, others by steaming. In my work with Sparta's ships, I have come to prefer a gentler approach, to maintain the integrity of the wood grain. So, we build troughs and fill them with fresh water; then the lengths of wood are laid in the troughs in the hot sunlight to soften them. In the meantime, I look around for the different vessels we need to mould those curves into the softened wood.

The construction of the biremes, which are the universally used warships of our time, gives them great strength, making the design ideal for the great horse of Troy. Essentially, the strength lies in the shell of the hull, which is then further reinforced by internal lateral ribs, locking into the keel that runs from bow to stern. The shell is a mortice and tenon construction, the planks being held together by a joint that is made up of two parts. The tenon portion of the joint works as a peg, and the mortice is the slot into which the tenon is inserted. This gives an extremely tight fit and prevents the hull from flexing too much. It requires many hours of precise carpentry, preceded by some intensive training and demonstrations, but my students are very attentive and seem to enjoy acquiring these highly specialised joinery skills. Walking around my small army of shipbuilders, I tell them that they should feel proud of their high-quality work.

Days and nights go by, and slowly the hull that will become the horse's back starts to rise from the sandy floor of the cave. Other groups are working on the head and neck, the legs and tail and the sled that must transport our secret weapon to its position. At one point, Epeios sees me taking a look at the cave entrance and coming to a decision. He nods. 'The final assembly will have to be outside, will it not?'

'Yes, sir. The horse will be far too tall to pass through.'

'I will lay on extra guards when that time comes.'

'And we will coat the entire structure with pitch to protect against any bad weather.'

*

It was while our pitch-black horse was being put together on the sands outside the cave that I became part of a conversation between Epeios and King Odysseus which cast as cold a shadow across me as did that sail the colour of a pale blood stain, when it first appeared on the horizon. By now, the king and the giant treated me as though I was, not their equal – which would have been uncomfortable – but a trusted vassal. So, they were seated, enjoying some wine, while they watched the final assembly, and I was rushing to and fro with ropes and orders for my team of horse-builders. We had constructed a pulley to hoist the body onto the legs and tail, with scaffolding and ladders to work from during the attachment. Then everyone settled to their tasks and King Odysseus called me over, offering me wine. Spartans hardly ever drink wine, because of the dangers and the shame of being drunk, but it would have seemed churlish to refuse, and I was greatly in need of the energy. So, I went and sat down with him and Epeios, and they continued their conversation, while I occasionally jumped up to solve an issue.

They were talking about the voyage home, in speculative terms. Epeios was concerned about the state of the ships. King Odysseus was more concerned about what the returning commanders would find when they reached their homeland after so long away. But, although I found out later that King Odysseus took years longer than any other commander to get home, and found his courageous wife fighting off an army of greedy suitors when he did, it was not of his concerns for himself that he was talking. It was about Agamemnon. As I sit down again and take a welcome sip of my wine, Odysseus is murmuring, 'His wife will never forgive him for sacrificing Iphigenia.'

Hearing that word, "sacrificing", my brain does a quick somersault. This, it says, *cannot* be about cutting his daughter's throat as a human sacrifice; it is a metaphor, perhaps for depriving her of a suitor. It *cannot* be about killing his own daughter.

After King Odysseus has returned to the camp, with torchlight now illuminating the hoisting of the head and neck onto the body, I ask Epeios, 'With respect, sir, what did King Odysseus mean about Agamemnon sacrificing his daughter? I mean, we do this with animals and chickens, but…'

Slowly, the giant turns his carved head towards me, the deep-set eyes carrying a glimmer of the torchlight. His soft voice says, 'Do you really want to know, young master shipbuilder?'

'I think I have to know, sir.'

'Then I will tell you. When men go to war, there is a rousing of bloodlust which, once begun, cannot be stopped. Do you know what bloodlust is?'

I shake my head.

'It is the only way that wars can be won. A hunger to kill, and kill, for the sake of killing.'

'But why did Agamemnon kill his own daughter? I don't understand!'

Epeios's huge head turns to look at the Aegean, the darkened waves whispering on the shore. 'At Aulis, more than one thousand Greek ships were massed. The cause of Helen had united the entire Greek world for the first time. Men were seething to go and fight, to conquer and avenge the insult that Paris had perpetrated. But no one could move, because there was no wind.'

'That's unusual for the Aegean.'

'Very unusual. It was taken as a bad omen. When the oracle was consulted, it emerged that Agamemnon had insulted Artemis by boasting that he could slay a deer better than she could.'

I can't stop the words. 'How childish of both of them!'

The slit eyes in the carved skull look back at me with a glint. 'Be careful what you say, master shipbuilder!'

'So, it was the oracle that told Agamemnon he must slaughter his child?'

'With these many thousands of men all desiring to do nothing else but fight and kill, things could have got out of hand if they could not sail to Troy. As far as Agamemnon was concerned, his credibility as a king and a general was at stake. It could be said that he had no choice.' Epeios gets to his feet, to summon more guards now that the great horse stands fully assembled. For a moment, we both look at this vast construction as its blackness makes a hole in the dying sunset. He concludes, 'Within the hour, the winds came.'

In my head, my silent voice replies, 'But they could have come anyway.'

*

The cold shadow of that conversation never left me. It haunted my dreams as well as my waking moments; whatever I was doing, it oppressed me almost physically, seeming to settle into the very air I was breathing, restrict my lungs and make my heart race. But although I could never put the memory behind me, the work had to go on.

Once the horse was assembled, I and twenty-nine volunteers carried out tests to make sure, firstly, that we could actually get thirty men of substantial height and build into the belly. Secondly, to check that the structure was taking the weight as it should do. Both of these tests yielded good results, with the mortice and tenon construction holding up well and very little flexing.

Then came the trial for the sled, with all this human cargo on board. We found that we needed more anchor points for the ropes, and the whole sled needed strengthening, by lashing more ropes front to rear and laterally. It took fifty men to pull the sled with the horse secured to it across the sand. Epeios looked on as they sweated and strained. 'It will take as many Trojans to pull it into Troy,' he observed, 'because although the going will not be soft as it is here, they will have those steep slopes to contend with.' King Odysseus attended the tests, and his hawklike eyes were approving. He gave the go-ahead for the horse to be moved to the Greek camp, which was already in the process of being cleared and the ships loaded, ready for the fire-raising that would follow.

Like Epeios, I had concerns for the seaworthiness of the Greek ships, after their long sojourn on the shores of Troy with no protection from the elements. But the time for any such thoughts was now past.

*

To my incredulity, I very nearly was not one of the thirty inside the horse. Spartans scorn anger as a kind of madness, but for once I found it hard to contain mine, as King Odysseus explained that the men had been hand-picked for their fighting prowess.

'Sir, what will they think if the creator of the horse is not one of them? That does not say much for my confidence in the wooden beast in which they are to penetrate Troy!'

A flash of something like respect crossed the king's dark eyes. 'That is well said, my young master shipbuilder. Very well, you shall be among them.'

So is he, of course, and Epeios, and the wronged husband, King Menelaus. Other royalty includes King Idomeneo of Crete with his right-hand man, Meriones. I would have thought that King Agamemnon, as the official leader of this whole enterprise, would have been one of our number, but he is not. I learned later that, during Agamemnon's bitter quarrel with Achilles over the slave girl Briseis, Achilles taunted him furiously for not leading his men from the front but instead remaining in the camp. Achilles' son Pyrrhos, naturally, is here with the fighting best of his Myrmidons.

Calchas the soothsayer is with us too, his presence presumably indicating that no bad omens threaten our success. That cold shadow haunts me again, as I remember the awful price of the voyage to Troy all those years ago, and I wonder if the price for this venture is yet to be paid. My fingers touch the metal of the sword and dagger with which they have armed me; I was aged seven when trained by the Spartan army to use such weapons. Through the slats of the neck and head structure I can see the night sky glowing orange with the flames of the burning camp. The ships have sailed, leaving only those that were too rotten to be used for anything but firewood.

It isn't long before we hear the voices of Trojans clamouring around us. And now, I feel cold sweat running down my back. If they sense that this is a trap, then spears will be mercilessly thrust inside the horse, fires lit beneath us and all will be over. There is much arguing in the torchlight. Then comes the sound of many more voices, and the horse jolts forward, creaking slightly; we are on the move.

In my mind's eye, I am watching as we cross the vast trench that barred our chariots. Onwards, through the palisade, and then through the gates into the lower city. The ground starting to rise, now, and the pace slowing, as men strain at the immense load. In here it is now swelteringly hot, but strict discipline prevails, and no one utters a sound, with not the faintest chink of a weapon. Upwards and ever upwards, towards the fifth line of defence, the outer wall of the citadel. We hear the mighty gates slowly open, with a scraping sound, and we pass through. Now, there is only one more line of defence: the inner wall of the citadel, protecting the palace. And now, the procession halts. Complete silence descends. It is clear that many Trojan soldiers have their ears to this wooden carcass that contains us. Every single one of them is listening. I try not to breathe. The stench of sweat and fear is so strong, I wonder that they can't smell it. If they decided to bring dogs, they would scent us in a flash, but, unlike many towns under siege, Troy has never used canines in its defences.

After an eternity, we hear a command given and the scraping sound again, as the mighty gates of the last, enormous wall of Troy swing open. A few minutes later, we have entered the citadel where lies the palace, together with what remains of the Trojan royal family and the stolen queen of King Menelaus. A Trojan priest is chanting, exhorting the people to give thanks to Athena and Apollo and to celebrate.

Pyrrhos is sitting opposite me, Myrmidons to either side of him. I wish I could see his face. At the sound of Apollo's name, I sense a slight movement from him; his fists are clenching. At the priest's words, is he thinking of Prince Hector's prophesy, as he lay dying in front of Achilles? 'I know what you are and was sure that I should not move you, for your heart is hard as iron; look to it that I bring not heaven's anger upon you on the day when Paris and Phoebus Apollo, valiant though you be, shall slay you at the Scaean gate.' Those were reportedly his words, and very shortly afterwards, Achilles died while valiantly scaling the main gate to the city; the Scaean gate was the one the Trojans used to exit the city and join battle with the Greeks on the plain below. The mightiest warrior in the Greek army had been hit in the heel by an arrow shot by Paris but – according to the soothsayer Calchas – guided by Apollo himself. Calchas went on to explain that the heel was the only vulnerable part of Achilles' body because when his mother, Thetis the goddess sea nymph, dipped her child in the River Styx to immortalise him, she held him by the heel.

Part of me is ready to believe that Paris's arrow was guided by Apollo, because Paris was a timid fighter, always holding back while brave Hector led from the front. Archers tend to be despised anyway, as they kill from a distance, shunning close-quarters combat, which the Greeks – especially the Spartans – actively seek. Paris himself met a fitting end when he was shot by our archer, Philoctetes.

Are these the scenes that are racing through Pyrrhos's mind as he sits with his fists clenched? Is this force that drives him, that makes him forget to eat and drink, a desperate desire for vengeance? But Paris is dead, a coward not fit to grovel in the dust before the man he killed. On whom, then, will Pyrrhos wreak vengeance? The gods themselves? All through the many hours while we listen to the carousing Trojans as they drink themselves into a stupor, these thoughts will not leave me.

*

Long after we can hear no more from the outside world, we continue to sit in silence. We know that, some hours ago, the Greek ships began their return under cover of darkness, alerted by the signalling of the spy who watched the gates of Troy open. It is still dark when King Odysseus gestures to me to release the hatch. I have oiled it so that it opens silently, first just a crack; more listening, then more opening; still, no sound from anywhere. Just as silently, the rope ladder is uncoiled. First down is Odysseus, followed by Pyrrhos and his men. I wait until everyone is safely descended, then slide down it. In time to see Pyrrhos running towards the tall towers of the palace, while the rest of the troops head for the gates. I follow them, hand on sword hilt; there is no telling how many guards we may encounter.

There are ten at the first inner gate, which secures the citadel; after a brief skirmish, they are dealt with, and the tall doors swing open. Then it's on down at a run to the outer gate, but this is unguarded, as are all other entrance points. And there on the plain, for once at the head of his army, is Agamemnon. We stand back as several thousand Greek soldiers run at full speed across the trench, into the lower city and up the hill towards the prize. Urgently, I follow them upwards. I desperately need to discover what havoc Pyrrhos is wreaking in the palace.

*

When Epeios talked of bloodlust, I found it hard to understand him. Spartan men are bred and trained for war, and fight in the army until they reach sixty, but our ethos is never to engage our emotions. We are not supposed to be angry in battle, and a Spartan who fights bravely but wishes to live is considered more honourable than one who does not care whether he lives or dies.

I will spare you the detail of what happened when we took Troy. Suffice it to say that no prisoners were taken. There was slaughter on a massive scale. All males were put to the sword and all females enslaved. I don't know how satisfied Pyrrhos was with his part in the bloodbath. Having cut down the aged King Priam, who had fled for sanctuary to the altar of Zeus, he threw Prince Hector's baby son Astyanax out of a turret window to his death.

And I can be very proud of what I have done. Because I am the architect of this horror.

*

Have you ever been locked into a nightmare from which you can't wake up and can't escape? It had begun to feel like that when I first heard about Iphigenia. Now, seeing this senseless slaughter, I wish I could go mad and not be aware of what is happening.

Then, Horror is joined by another companion; we will call him the Absurd, who often arrives in a timely way in the choicest nightmares. And it is enough to make me feel some hope that I might really be going mad. The Greeks have turned the palace inside out; they have smashed chests, knocked down walls and tortured slaves for information. They have desecrated temples, ripping down tapestries and dismantling altars. Then they have gone house by house through the lower city, tearing everything apart. They have looked for escape tunnels; they have even returned to the charred remains of their camp and shovelled through the ruins. But, dead or alive, Helen is nowhere to be found.

While the rank and file are sent to complete the sacking of the city, their leaders gather in the throne room for a hastily convened conference, presided over by Agamemnon. Present are Menelaus, the husband who is still without his wife; King Idomeneo of Crete and his right-hand man, Meriones; King Odysseus and Epeios; Calchas the soothsayer; and, for reasons that I don't understand but don't care anyway, myself. Pyrrhos is not present; I imagine he is busy sacking with his Myrmidons.

Agamemnon is looking thunderous. Hand on sword, he turns to Calchas – the same soothsayer who told the king how he could bring the winds to sail to this place by cutting his daughter's throat. Thin and ragged-looking, the man is trembling; I daresay he foresaw that he would get the blame for this. 'You knew, didn't you? Admit it! This is treachery, you wretch!'

The soothsayer is silent with terror, merely shaking his head. But King Odysseus steps forward, putting a restraining hand on Agamemnon's arm. 'Put up your sword, King, and be calm. I have something to say to you all, but it will be done over some choice Trojan wine.' Orderlies have appeared out of nowhere, carrying flagons and goblets and providing seating for those assembled. And I realise that the wily king of Ithaca has seen this coming and prepared for it.

With spirits having been as inflamed as they were ever going to be, the wine acts as a sedative. The men sit down, taking appreciative gulps from gold cups, and look around them at the captured glory of the royal palace. And King Odysseus takes centre stage, walking from time to time towards this member of the audience or that, as if he were reciting an epic poem. But he does not declaim as might a traditional poet. Rather, in his quiet, dry voice, it is as though he is sharing a secret in total confidence with those assembled. His words, aided no doubt by the wine, have a mesmerising effect on his audience. But no eyes start to close; all are fixed on the king of Ithaca who, like them, has come many miles and spent many years to arrive in this throne room, at this moment.

'You will recall,' says King Odysseus, 'that Queen Helen was abducted while her husband was away in Crete, conducting the obsequies of his grandfather. Abandoning her daughter Hermione, then nine years old, and taking many valuables with her, she fled with Paris, it was thought, to his native city of Troy.

'When you, King Menelaus, discovered how gravely you had been dishonoured and your hospitality abused, you came to your brother at Mycenae and urged him to muster an army against Troy and to raise levies in Greece. He, sending a herald to each of the kings, reminded them of the oaths of fealty they had sworn and warned them to look to the safety of their own wives, saying that the affront had been offered equally to the whole of Greece.

'And thus it was that eleven hundred or more ships sailed to Troy: the first time, quite possibly, that the whole of the Greek world had united against a common enemy.' He pauses to take some wine, while audience members nod to each other in agreement at the memories they all share.

King Odysseus continues in the same calm voice: 'Nine years is a long time. So it is possible that not everyone will recall that when you made landfall at Troy and demanded the return of Queen Helen and the plunder, the reply came that neither had ever been in Troy; both were in Egypt, under the guardianship of the Pharaoh.'

Agamemnon now interjects: 'And who in their right mind would ever have believed that story!'

Odysseus acknowledges the comment with a slight bow and continues, 'Of course, the story could neither be proved nor disproved except by sacking Troy.'

At that point, the quiet voice in my head murmurs, 'They could have verified the story nine years ago by a visit to Egypt.' But it is doubtless more than my life is worth to utter such words. And it would utterly destroy the diplomacy with which Odysseus is weaving a web of enchantment round his audience.

The king continues, 'Troy has been sacked and Queen Helen is not here. Neither, it is likely, is the plunder. And I have managed to elicit information from various sources about what actually happened when she and the scoundrel Paris absconded from the palace at Sparta. It would appear that their ship was blown off course in a storm and ended up in the western Nile Delta. Here, Paris's men abandoned him, went straight to the nearest Egyptian authorities and reported that Paris was a kidnapper, a thief and an adulterer who was on the run. The authorities sent messages to Pharaoh asking what to do, and he wrote back, requesting that Paris be brought before him.

'Pharaoh questioned Paris as to his journey and what had actually happened at Sparta. He also questioned the crew, and when their stories did not match, Pharaoh determined that Paris was lying. He ordered him and his men to leave Egypt within three days. But not with Helen, and not with the plunder; both would remain in Egypt to be kept safe until they could be returned to Menelaus. And there they await him.'

King Odysseus ceases and seats himself. There is a long silence. Then King Idomeneo of Crete says, 'Surely we had sightings of Helen on the castle walls?'

Epeios says in his soft voice, 'From that kind of distance, any woman could have seemed to be Helen. We see what we want to see.'

Odysseus adds, almost casually, 'I have also heard that in the Egyptian city of Memphis on the Nile Delta, there is a temple dedicated to the "foreign Aphrodite"; no other temples in Egypt have been dedicated to foreign deities.'

Menelaus's tone has a quiet finality that draws a line under the conversation. 'It was essential that the coward Paris be punished by death for rupturing the ancient laws of hospitality and abducting a queen. It was essential that Troy be punished for harbouring him. All this has been done. Now that we are avenged, I will hasten to Egypt and return with my queen to Sparta.' He bows to Agamemnon. 'And I thank you from my heart, brother, for the mighty alliance you summoned to my aid. The Greek world has triumphed over the barbarians who would have made us eat dust!'

That night, I run all the way to the beach to sleep on one of our ships. And despite my efforts to get as far away as possible from the Horror and the Absurd, all night the two Furies scream with laughter that seems to reach to the stars above; as dawn breaks, the shrieking is still there. I have nights even now when I hear that laughter again.

*

This sense of being helplessly bound in an unending nightmare drags on through the following days and nights. Not because of the sacking of the city and the removal of everything of value onto the ships. Nor because of the enslavement of Hector's wife Andromache, along with Hecuba, the widowed wife of King Priam, and her daughters Cassandra and Polyxena. But because, once more, the winds are against the Greeks.

Gone are the Etesians that we need to carry us southwards and home and to take Menelaus to Egypt. Every day, I watch as a moaning gale blows hard onshore, raising angry twelve-foot waves and pinning us helplessly on the beach. That cold horror I felt when Epeios told me about Iphigenia grips my heart. And I gaze out across the stormy sea and shout to Poseidon to take me, if it will make the gods feel any better. I don't feel that I deserve to be alive, when innocents have been slaughtered because of my invention.

Finally, inevitably, another meeting is convened in the throne room. Those present are the same as before but with the addition of Pyrrhos, who has brought two of his Myrmidons for good measure. I wonder if he was asked to attend or if he invited himself. He comes to stand beside me;

I can feel the tension in him, like I could sense his clenched fists when we were in the horse.

King Odysseus once again leads the meeting, and he too is looking far from relaxed. The relentless wind moaning and buffeting around the windows provides a suitable background accompaniment as he begins: 'For ten days now, we have been ready to sail for our homes, yearning for all we left behind when we set off for Troy. And for ten days, the winds have been onshore and unseasonably strong, imprisoning us in this foreign land.' He looks around the assembly. 'It has to be asked if, as was the case in Aulis, a god is angry with us, if some grave offence has been committed. And so I have asked Calchas to use his divining skills to enlighten us. He has done so.' The voice of King Odysseus now has a warning note. 'And I would ask you all to remember that the words of the soothsayer are not his own; they come from the gods, and they flatter no one.' He turns to Calchas and, with a kindlier tone, says: 'I thank you, Calchas, for assisting us in this matter, and I guarantee your safety: anyone who wishes you harm will have to answer to me.'

Calchas bows his head in acknowledgement. He is wearing a purple cloak with a gold clasp and looks very different to the ragged, trembling wretch who stood accused by Agamemnon of misleading the Greek army. 'I thank you, my lord, for these assurances.'

Odysseus says briskly, 'What Calchas has to say will take a little time. So, I mean you all to be as comfortable as possible and to pay close attention.' He claps his hands, and – in a mirror image of the first meeting – orderlies enter with seating and wine.

When everyone is settled, Calchas speaks in measured tones: 'My lords, the heart of this business begins with the death of Hector, when he was slain by Achilles.' Next to me, Pyrrhos clenches his fists. Calchas continues, 'You will recall that Prince Achilles did not leave the remains of Hector on the battlefield; instead, he attached them to his chariot and dragged them round the city walls. This happened repeatedly over a number of days.'

Pyrrhos growls, 'And where is the offence in that?'

Odysseus was evidently expecting this interjection, because he says calmly to the young warrior, 'There was no offence to the gods in that, Prince; Calchas has not yet arrived at the point of his story. Pray listen, and be calm.'

I can feel anger like heat radiating from Pyrrhos's body as Calchas continues: 'One night, Achilles was astonished to receive a visitor. Disguised as a beggar, in filthy rags, the ageing King Priam had somehow managed to gain access to the Greek camp and slip unobserved to Achilles' hut. Once there, he threw himself on Achilles' mercy and under his protection as a host. And he begged Achilles to give him Hector's remains so that he might give his son an honourable burial.'

Calchas pauses and I find myself looking at Menelaus; his eyes hold a dawning knowledge – he knows where this is going. Next to me, Pyrrhos's fists are still tightly clenched, his breathing shallow.

'Prince Achilles,' continues Calchas, 'showed himself to be a prince of mercy that night. He fulfilled every duty that, under the law of Zeus, the protector of strangers, he was obliged to do. He gave the old king food and wine and a bed of soft animal skins to rest his weary bones. In the early hours of the morning, he laid the shrouded body of Hector in a cart and personally escorted King Priam to the gates of the camp. He also promised the old king that a truce would be held for fourteen days, to allow the Trojans to celebrate the funeral games of their prince. As you all will doubtless recall, that truce held.'

Calchas pauses again, then finds the words to go on. 'Under the ancient laws of hospitality, once a stranger has been placed under the protection of his host, that protection must stand forever. If the host is absent, due to death or any other reason, then the host's nearest kin are under the same obligation. When we entered Troy, King Priam was cut down by the son of Achilles at the altar of Zeus, to which he had fled for sanctuary. A great and ancient law has been violated, and at the very altar of Zeus, the king of gods, and the protector of the stranger. It is Zeus himself who has commanded the winds to imprison us here.'

The soothsayer concludes, and that icy horror grips my heart once again. I stare at the mosaics of the tiles beneath my feet, depicting dancers, wine and flowers. As I raise my eyes, I see that everyone is looking at Pyrrhos. He draws his sword, and his men do the same. His deep voice is a savage growl. 'Am I to be punished for avenging my father's death at the hands of the Trojans?'

More hands move to sword hilts. Then King Odysseus speaks with his usual calm authority. 'Put up your sword, noble son of Achilles. It is not your blood that is required in sacrifice to Zeus.'

Slowly, Pyrrhos and his men sheathe their swords. Odysseus nods to Calchas, who takes his cue: 'It has been determined that a slave prized by the Greeks will provide a fitting sacrifice.'

Pyrrhos snarls, 'Then let it be Princess Polyxena! If my father had lived, she would have been his prize. Let her join him in death!'

At this point, the cacophony of screams and laughter that has been haunting me breaks my head apart with such violence that I have no further memory of the meeting.

*

Keen to keep up the momentum that would carry the Greeks home on a favourable wind, Agamemnon ordered that the sacrifice should take place without delay. While an altar was being hastily built on the shore near the ships, I walked, sick to the heart, that dreadful clamour in my head, to the cave where we had built the horse. Some unused planks were still lying around. I seized an axe and hacked mindlessly at the wood, until sharp pieces flew around, striking me in the face and arms and drawing blood. I kept on and on, until blood was streaming down my arms. And still, it was not enough.

I spent that night in the cave. It seemed the only place where I could seek some kind of innocence, find the person I was before I built the horse. But, while I knew that the slaughter of Princess Polyxena was taking place on that beach, there was no innocence and no sleep for me. I was bloody with the guilt of building the creation that had brought all this horror.

The following morning, as daylight started to creep into the cave, I knew immediately. Walking along the beach, I could feel the warm wind pushing my back. The sky had cleared of storm clouds. The Etesians had returned to sail us home. But I could feel no joy in this. I felt nauseated, as though I could never swallow food or drink again.

When we came to boarding the ships for Sparta, I chose the sorriest one I could find, with rotting ribs and a ragged sail. With the number of ships that were found to be unseaworthy and burned when the fleet sailed for Tenedos, this poor wreck was heavily overloaded.

Dense smoke is coiling into the air from the burning city on the tall hill, as our fleet of pitch-black ships sets sail for home. With every oar taken on this vastly overcrowded vessel, I stand at the stern and watch until what remains of Troy can be seen no more.

TWO

BLACK SAND

The sail of this wretched craft being largely in tatters, most of our progress is down to the oarsmen, who pull with the energy of men perishing to see their homeland again. At first, I note, without surprise, that seawater is leaking freely through the seams of the ship's longitudinal members. My hope is that, in time, the wood will swell as it takes up water, and the leaks will be stemmed. As days and nights go by, at first with much bailing by the lower deck crew, the leaks slow, although they do not entirely abate.

The Etesian winds give us a steady, fast blow southwards, past Skyros and as far as the peninsula from where, on that fateful day of the first sacrifice of a young girl, the Greek ships sailed out of Aulis. Up to this stage, the fleet largely remains together, or as far as I can see, anyway, with sails billowing to the far horizons. But now, many ships – including those of Agamemnon – are leaving the fleet to return to their point of departure. I remember the words of Odysseus to Epeios: "his wife will never forgive him for sacrificing Iphigenia". And I wonder what kind of welcome the child-killing king of Mycenae will find.

As soon as we leave the wide open North Aegean Sea and approach the Cyclades islands, the winds become fickler and the fleet is inevitably dispersed. Island sailing is a tricky business, with katabatic winds created by the varying contours and temperatures of the islands' mountains and valleys. But it is only when we race past an island dominated by a black, conical mountain with beaches of black sand, an island that I have never seen before, it is only then that I realise – we have been carried far off-course, to the south-east of the Peloponnesus, and Sparta is now to the north of us. And still we hurtle southwards, leaving my homeland further and further behind.

Several hours later, I think I can see the mountainous outline of a large island ahead of us. But at that same moment, a squall of intense ferocity strikes, with powerful gusts whipping up ten-foot waves. In no time, the gale becomes a storm of epic proportions. The sky darkens as ragged, black clouds race across, the wind propelling us forwards at a terrifying speed. With what is left of the sail reefed, we are still in serious trouble, trying to keep our battered ship heading into the waves. Then I see what I have been dreading: water is pouring through seams that are bending and sagging. Our overloaded ship is giving up. Shouting to the men, 'We must lighten the load!', I start to hurl bags of plunder overboard. But, more concerned about losing their precious booty than their lives, the fools threaten me at knifepoint. In the tiny second that their knives flash in front of my throat, glinting in a sudden crack of lightning, something snaps inside me. Running to the stern, I dive into the sea. At least now the ship will be lighter by the weight of a man.

*

As soon as I enter the water, I find the peace that I have been seeking so desperately for so long. I don't try and swim; no one can fight waves this huge. I lie on my back, from time to time completely submerged by tall, curling crests and lashing spray. Looking up at the lightning spitting from the black clouds ballooning across the heavens. Hearing the boom of thunder. And thanking Poseidon for sending his Furies to destroy mine, drowning the hideous spectres that have wrecked my peace of mind ever since I first heard about the tragedy of Iphigenia. There is no more place for these horrors in my head; it is full of thunder, lightning, gales and salt water. I feel like a newborn child, being rocked in its mother's arms, powerless and, at last, innocent. I pray to Poseidon to take me while I am in this state of happiness; it will be a wonderful way to die.

*

All sounds now fade except for the rushing of water, and I suppose that I must be under the sea. So Poseidon is answering my prayers. Soon all my troubles will be over. I do not feel the need to breathe. Suddenly, in the blackness of the water, arms wrap round my body and start pulling me upwards. I contemplate resisting but find that I have no strength left for anything. As if in a dream, I am dragged and tugged until my head breaks through the surface and into the storm-filled air. As soon as I am above the surface, the coughing and retching start; I might be happy to have my lungs filling with water, but my lungs are not. With a bump I am landed like a fish on the beach, and the hands that took me from the waves now start pummelling the water out of my chest. Those first tiny gasps of air are like those of a child that has been pulled from a womb that did not want to give him up. They are acutely painful, and they are godsent. Panting like a runner at the end of his race, I pass into a sleep that is not going to be the death of me.

When I wake, the storm has passed, and the bright sun is warming my skin. I am lying on a shore of black sand, small blue waves lapping at my feet. Next to me, a sea nymph kneels in the sand, golden hair dripping down her soaking robe. I can't make out her face, as the sun is shining from behind her, making a halo from her wet hair. She is holding a flagon. When I struggle to find the strength to sit up, she slides an arm round my back and raises me, holding the flagon to my lips. It is warm and sweet with honey. When I have taken some, she gets up and goes to a dainty grey mare that has been standing patiently behind us. Lifting a saddlebag from the mare's back, my rescuer reaches inside it and brings out a small cake. Kneeling back down, she lifts me and feeds me like a baby. It is a kind of honey bread, more delicious than I have ever tasted; I wonder if I am dead and have passed into Paradise after all. When I have eaten all of the cake, she gently lies me back down and my heavy eyelids close, my mouth full of sweetness instead of salt water.

When I wake again, the sea nymph is still kneeling at my side. I am aware of sea-blue eyes gazing at me with a blazing intensity, but I am too dazzled to look for long. I have never been so close to beauty before; it makes me dizzy. Now that I can feel some strength returning, I struggle to my knees and bow to her. With a voice hoarse from coughing, I mumble, 'Gracious lady, I owe you my life. How can I ever repay you?'

She stands, holding out a hand to help me up. 'When your strength has returned, you will be given many ways to thank me, merman. Come – do you think you can get on Petra?'

I have never ridden a horse. 'I will be very clumsy. I hope she won't mind…'

'She's very tolerant.' She takes the mare's bridle, talking to her gently, while I scramble weakly aboard.

The sea nymph leads us along the shore until the sun is high in the sky. The imprints from the mare's hooves in the black sand fill with water from the ripples of the Aegean, where Poseidon now peacefully slumbers. She says, 'I often walk this shore. I was there when the storm broke. I saw your poor ship. Where she sank, the water was very deep. Then, I saw you floating towards the shore and disappearing. You were headed for rocks.'

She takes me to a cave along that black shore, where the waves wash into the first part, then the ground rises, and it is dry. Petra splashes happily into the cave and up onto the dry sand, as though she has been here before. On the sand is a bed of animal skins, a flask and a dish with more honey bread. I slide off the little mare, and my rescuer takes my arm until I can lie, exhausted, on the bed. Kneeling beside me again, she says, 'You must eat and drink and sleep. You will be safe here; no one will come. Tomorrow, I will return, and we will talk.' I badly want to talk now, but my eyelids are already closing.

When I wake next, the seawater in the cave reflects the silver light of the moon, in a long pathway that seems to lead out of the cave and onwards towards the horizon. There is not a sound except for the gentle murmur of the Aegean. I drink some of the honeyed water and sleep again.

Dawn is casting a rose-coloured glow on the ancient cave walls when my eyes open again. The air is fresh and cool with sea breezes. Feeling hunger as I have not felt it in a long time, I attack the honey bread like a starving animal. More gulps of the honeyed water, and I feel my strength flooding back. I stand, look around me, then walk to the cave entrance and look out at the shore. Just next to the cave an old fig tree is growing, well furnished with fruit. But I would not dream of taking any. On this enchanted isle, it would be showing disgraceful ingratitude for the life-saving hospitality already shown to me.

The horizon is empty of any sail, and there is no sign of wreckage from the poor ship that went down. Wary of being observed, I return to the comforting bowels of the cave and explore further inside. My attention is caught by a shaft of sunlight that must be entering through a hole in the cave roof. Walking towards it, I come to a set of seven steps leading downwards and stop in surprise; they are obviously man-made. Cautiously, I descend and proceed along a passageway that rises gradually into a chamber. The shaft of light is shining directly onto a rectangular stone altar. Next to the altar is a pedestal, or worship stone, which would have held a statue of the deity being venerated. And next to that are two cylindrical stalagmites rising from the floor of the cave, one considerably taller than the other. In the gentle beam of light, they look for all the world like the figures of a mother and child. Moved by the scene, I bow my head in respect to whatever deity this may be and back out of the chamber.

As I re-enter the main part of the cave, there is a sudden faint rumbling that makes the air around me vibrate. I hurry to the cave entrance. The distant thunder continues. And now I see a column of dark smoke on the horizon. It reminds me of my last sight of Troy. The rumbling finally ceases. But the smoke is still rising to the sky when I see Petra and her mistress in the distance on the beach. I go back into the cave to await their arrival, conscious that I must not be seen.

She dismounts outside the cave and leads Petra inside. The golden hair no longer streams down damp clothes but is braided in a gleaming crown around her head. She wears a simple white dress that billows gently in the sea breeze. She looks approvingly at the empty dish. 'You are a different person, merman. Sleep has been good for you.'

'I feel like a new man, my lady. Ready to hear how I can be of help to you.'

She smiles and puts down a bag next to the plate. 'Here is some meat to put more flesh on your bones. You can eat while I speak. Then it will be your turn.'

It seems disrespectful to eat the meat and bread she has brought, while she has nothing in front of her. But I am becoming accustomed to doing as this goddess tells me. She seats herself on a rock, occasionally feeding Petra some small pieces of honey bread, which the mare delicately takes from her hand.

She begins, 'I feel that your story and mine are like two worlds gradually moving together, until they revolve around each other. You had better prepare for the fact that we have both shared some experiences which have changed us forever.'

But I could never have prepared for what she was to tell me.

'I am a daughter of King Agamemnon. My name is Chrysothemis. My younger brother is Orestes. My older sister is Electra. And once, I had an oldest sister called Iphigenia, whom I loved dearly. She was always very sweet to me, although I must have been an annoying little sister! She let me dress up in her fine clothes and her jewellery. If she was at a feast which I was too young to attend, she would save the choicest morsels for me, bring them up to my bedroom and tell me funny stories about how silly people had been.'

Princess Chrysothemis pauses, and I now know what has changed her forever.

In a calm voice, she continues: 'When the winds would not blow for the Greek ships to sail to Troy, my father knew that my mother would never let Iphigenia be sacrificed, as the soothsayer had decreed. So, he practised the cruellest deception possible. He sent a message saying that she was to be married to Prince Achilles, the finest warrior of all the Greeks. She was to come to Aulis, where her prince awaited her.' The blue eyes turn to me. 'Did you know of this deception, merman?'

'No, my lady.'

'My sister felt that all her dreams were coming true. She had heard of Achilles and adored the very idea of him. She and my mother immediately set about packing her finest robes and jewellery. Electra was very quiet; she said afterwards that it was because she had a foreboding. I think she was jealous.'

Princess Chrysothemis pauses again, and I gently ask: 'How did you feel about your sister's marriage to Achilles, my lady?'

'I was eight years old. I was thrilled for my beautiful sister. When Achilles heard how his name had been brought into the deception, he was very angry. He wanted to fight to protect Iphigenia. But even his own Myrmidons were against him, along with the entire Greek army. And that is when Iphigenia herself intervened. She said she did not want Achilles to be killed trying to defend her; she would go willingly to be sacrificed if it would help the cause of the Greeks. And so, the sacrifice went ahead. And the winds returned.'

Princess Chrysothemis holds out another morsel to Petra and strokes her mane. 'When my mother discovered that her eldest daughter had been butchered on the altar like a sacrificial goat, her anger can barely be imagined. Electra told me she knew from that moment that Queen Clytemnestra would have her revenge. She would kill King Agamemnon when he returned. And then, Electra said, our little brother Orestes would have to avenge his father by killing his mother. In fact, Electra feared so much that Clytemnestra's hunger for revenge would extend to her own son as well as her husband, that she arranged for Orestes to be sent away to be schooled in Athens. And from the moment she heard of the death of Iphigenia, Electra went into mourning.'

Dimly, in the back of my head, I can hear that screaming laughter.

Her voice steady, Princess Chrysothemis continues: 'It took years for me to really understand what had happened and what was going to happen. This dreadful, unending cycle of revenge. Even now, my father must have arrived home. Even now, his wife is planning his death. Two years ago, I decided that I could not be part of this anymore. The whole course of my life was to be caught up in a tragedy of others' making. So, I ran away. Gathering up what few pieces of jewellery I had, I went in the early hours of the morning to the port and bribed a fisherman to take me here, to Crete.'

Crete. I had been wondering; now I know. 'That was a long and dangerous voyage!'

'It was terrifying. I hope the poor man survived the journey back.'

'What did you do once you were ashore?'

'I threw myself on the mercy of King Idomeneo; he was at the war, fighting alongside my father. But it suited his wife to take me in. There is always rivalry between Greek kings, and I suppose she thought I could become a pawn in her husband's game.'

'Has King Idomeneo now returned?'

'Not yet. I was looking out for his ship when I saw yours.' She gestures to the plate of meat and bread. 'You must eat – you are very thin!'

'I can only eat if you do too, my lady.'

'Very well!' So, we share the food and I have never had a more enjoyable meal.

*

Once the last crumbs have been consumed, Princess Chrysothemis looks at me with kindly eyes. 'Now, merman, I have told you my name. Will you tell me yours and where you are from?'

'It is Damian, my lady. I am a Spartan.'

'Enough of "my lady". You must call me Chryso – Iphigenia always did.'

'I will try, my lady… Chryso.'

'It could be as hard for me not to call you merman, but you are not, are you? What happened in Troy that made you want to drown?'

'I made the horse that carried the Greeks into the city to murder old men and children and to sacrifice Princess Polyxena.'

She murmurs, 'Those who have already returned told of a great horse.' She looks at me with those startlingly blue eyes. 'How did you know how to make such a thing?'

'I was trained by my father to be a shipbuilder.'

Chryso's reaction is not at all what I would have expected. She claps her hands with delight, and the little mare tosses her head in surprise. 'You can build ships! Wonderful!'

At that moment, the distant rumble comes again, and the air vibrates. I go to the mouth of the cave and look across the sea. The dark column of smoke rises to the cloudy skies. Returning to Chryso, who is soothing the nervous mare, I ask, 'Is that sound something to do with the Minotaur?'

Chryso laughs quietly. 'Oh, King Idomeneo would love all who come here to believe that!'

'I thought Theseus dispatched the beast.'

Chryso looks at me with her head on one side. 'Let us discuss this beast, shall we? A monster, a man with the head of a bull? A monster that demands to be fed on human flesh? And yet no word has ever come down from a single human being who has actually seen this creature. We only have Theseus's word for it that he actually slew a monster. I think he was an unreliable witness and fatally absent-minded, in forgetting to lower the black sail and hoist a white one on his return, which caused his poor old father, Aegeus, to drown himself in the sea that is now named after him. I do believe that bit; it has a ring of truth to it.'

'And it was all very long ago; so, what is that rumbling?'

'Don't let us dismiss the Minotaur yet. But the story seemed to originate at a time when Athens was coming into prominence in the Greek world and needed a bully-boy hero.'

Chryso stands, so I do too. 'I have to go now. They expect me to wait on them at table at supper times. Keeps me in my place.'

'You are treated as a slave!'

She smiles. 'Not really. I have a great deal of freedom during the day. The waiting at table is just to point out that I am not worthy of eating with them. I would rather eat with the servants, and it's so easy to get spare food. Until tomorrow!'

'Until tomorrow, my lady Chryso.'

Laughing at my new title for her, she leads Petra from the cave.

*

As the sun sinks, I take a dip in the Aegean, thinking it unlikely that anyone will be observing me now. I float on my back, like I did after I dived from the wreck. Only this time, the moon goddess sends her silver to soothe me with tiny waves. Selene's glow infuses my dreams that night; I had never thought that it would be possible to feel as peaceful as this.

I sleep so deeply that the next morning, Chryso gently shakes me awake. The high sun is blazing into the cave. She brings more honey bread and meat, with a new flask of honeyed water. I struggle up. 'How was the waiting at table last night, my lady?'

Her voice is not quite as calm as it was. 'King Idomeneo has returned. He brings news that my father King Agamemnon has been murdered by my mother, his wife, Clytemnestra, and her lover, Aegisthus.'

As the spectral figures in my head start their screaming laughter, I ask, 'Does this put you in danger, my lady?'

'It will now turn his attention to me, as his guest, his slave or his hostage. I do not know which.'

I look at her brilliant blue eyes for a slightly longer time than I normally can. 'But you have a plan, don't you, my lady Chryso?'

She says, 'Have you found the altar at the back of this cave? Where the sunbeams shine in?'

'Yes. What deity was worshipped there?'

'Eileithyia, the goddess of fertility. Shall we go and pay our respects?'

I follow her to the sunlit chamber where the beams fall on the altar and illuminate the strange mother and child stalagmites next to it. Chryso says softly, 'This a very ancient chamber of worship. It is no longer visited now, which is why I knew you would be safe in this cave.' She kneels in front of the altar, and I kneel with her.

She says, 'You know of the ancient demand from King Minos for seven young couples from Athens to come yearly to Crete and be given to the Minotaur?'

I nod.

'It was said that this was a penance for Athens having murdered a son of Minos, in jealousy at his achievements at their games. You remember that?'

'I do, my lady.'

She stands, and I follow her back into the main part of the cave. 'Every year, more couples still come here. But I think that the Minotaur story is a cover-up. Crete was, my history tutors said, once a thalassocracy, its trading ships and warships dominating the Aegean. As Athens came to prominence, she must have seen Crete as her main rival. But they came to a trade deal; I don't doubt that Crete pays Athens handsomely for the couples they send. And they do not die; they are kept as prisoners for one purpose only.'

'Why does Crete need these young couples?'

Her voice is gentle. 'In some countries, couples have difficulties bearing children. I think that this has always been the case here in Crete.'

'Why would that be?'

The distant rumble comes again. Chryso says, 'Something in the air we breathe? The food we eat? The water we drink? Whatever the reason, no king of Crete would ever have wanted it broadcast throughout the Greek world that his people were struggling to bear children!'

'So, these couples are imprisoned in the labyrinth?'

She nods. 'Until they produce one or more children. Then, they are given homes in the mountain communities, under strict orders never to say where they have come from.'

'How did you discover all this, my lady?'

'Like you, I wondered at the rumbling from across the horizon and the column of smoke as well. The servants who I ate with in the evenings told me it was the monster. They had seen the young couples arriving under guard and being taken down into the labyrinth. As it lies directly beneath the palace, they could hardly have missed the event. They said none of the Athenians were ever seen again.' A look flashes across Chryso's face that I have seen before, determination as limitless as the grains of sand on which we are standing.

She continues: 'I decided to see for myself just what inhabited those underground passages.'

I am holding my breath, expecting her to recount what she found, when she smiles at me, amused. 'As you can see, I survived the experience! Now, I am not required to wait at table tonight – I think that King Idomeneo wishes to discuss with his wife what must become of me. So, at sunset I will come for you, and we will go to the palace and descend together into the labyrinth.'

THREE
THE BULL LEAPER

The palace of Knossos towers over the Aegean, with its heavily guarded port beneath, thronging with trading ships coming and going and with hundreds of sheds along the port sides housing its many warships.

The palace itself is three stories high and gracefully built; beneath, another three stories down, lies the plethora of workrooms and storerooms, linked by adjoining doors and endless winding passages, that is known as the labyrinth.

On the way there, Chryso explains that there is no danger of us encountering any guards in the labyrinth itself, as King Idomeneo's soldiers, like his servants, are terrified of the monstrous beast with the body of a man and the head of a bull. There are guards who patrol the perimeter, but Chryso knows how often they pass by and how to slip through.

And so, as the sun descends in crimson fire below the Aegean, Chryso lights her torch, and we begin our journey downwards into the underworld of the palace of Knossos. I am considerably surprised at the height of the tunnel, but the real surprises begin as we round a corner and see the torchlight shine on a glory of shimmering colour. The exquisite fresco depicts two young men carrying amphorae. But these youths are like none I have ever seen. Slender-waisted, their long, dark hair curling around their shoulders, each with a graceful, upright spine, embroidered loin cloth and muscular torso rippling with effortless, proud movement. I whisper, 'These young men are more like gods than Greeks! Who are they, my lady?'

She says softly, 'I think, a people from long, long ago. But there is more…'

Round the next corner, and we could be looking at three queens, their dark hair elegantly coiffed and adorned with pearls. Stunned, I hardly dare to gaze at them, so assured is their demeanour.

The next fresco depicts four magnificent dolphins engaged in a kind of dance with smaller fish, so true to life and with colours so vibrant – terracotta red and Aegean blue – I half expect them to swim towards us. And all these wonderful depictions are simply bursting with the joy of life. These do not look like a people who engage in endless, futile wars with each other. Who practise the human sacrifice of young girls. And throw babies out of high windows. I can feel tears stinging my eyes. If I could have lived with these people, my father would still be alive. And Iphigenia. And Polyxena. And Astyanax.

But it is the final fresco, around another corner in the twisting passageways that go forever downwards, which amazes me most of all. Chryso shines her torch on a mighty bull, with curving, powerful contours. He is in full charge, but his horns are being firmly gripped by a youth who slows his movement, while his colleague is somersaulting down the creature's back in a move of spectacular athleticism. Another youth waits with outstretched arms at the animal's rear to catch the bull leaper. My heart almost stops as I gaze at the magnificent head and curving neck of this extraordinary force of nature and at the humans who look as though they are playing with him. 'The Minotaur…'

Chryso shines the torch around the sumptuous colours of the fresco. 'That is what successive kings of Crete wanted everyone to think. But this is no half-man, half-animal monster, is it?'

I say quietly, 'The bull is beautiful. And I do not think that the bull leapers want to harm it. It's like a game.' As we descend further, there is another ground-shaking rumbling.

I ask Chryso, 'How did you find your way out of this place? There was no Ariadne thread for you!'

'I have a good memory; it really was not difficult to put the left and right-hand turns into reverse.'

'And the Athenians who are imprisoned down here, are there wardens who bring them food and drink?'

'The wardens live down here too. Every day, food and drink supplies are left at the entrance.'

'So, could the wardens catch us on our way in or out?'

'Not at night. And if they do see us down there, they will assume that we are simply one of the Athenian couples.'

'Has anyone ever tried to escape?'

She shakes her head. 'They are terrified at the thought of the Minotaur.'

'And yet, you have been to see them many times unscathed?'

Chryso looks at me. 'When you have been a prisoner for so long, the thought of breaking out into the world again can be terrifying.'

'Is that what you are going to offer them?'

'Yes. And this is where you come into it, Damian. How do you feel about building a ship in which we can all sail away?'

*

As we approach a row of doors in the right-hand wall, Chryso whispers, 'I speak mostly with Pericles and his wife; they pass the word round to the other couples. Their rooms are too small to gather in.' She taps gently on the first door we come to, whispering, 'Your friend!'

The door is opened by a strikingly handsome young man, who smiles immediately he sees Chryso, and then at me. 'Gracious lady, and your friend, please come in!'

Inside a small, sparsely furnished room, a beautiful young girl offers us seats; she looks no more than fourteen years old. Chryso gives her a hug. 'Athena, Pericles, this is Damian. He has been at Troy and survived.'

Athena presses drinks of honeyed water on us and we cannot refuse. We all sit, Athena and Pericles looking intently at me. And I have the sudden thought, *on no account must I let these people down!*

Chryso says quietly, 'The only way to get you all out of here is to leave Crete far behind. The port is far too heavily guarded for us to steal a ship. But Damian knows how to build ships!'

Pericles' eyes glow. 'The men will all help, working under your instructions!'

Athena's reply is cautious: 'That is wonderful! But where can we flee to?'

Pericles tells me, 'We will not be welcome back in Athens; they received much gold in return for us.'

Chryso glances at me; she knows I have the answer. I look at Pericles, feeling as familiar with him already as I would with an old friend. 'If you and your men are willing to join the Spartan army, that is where we can go!'

Chryso starts to plan. 'The shipbuilding must happen at night. I can take all the tools we need from the workrooms down here. What types of wood do you want, Damian?'

'Oak for the outer shell. Softwoods such as cypress for the interior. And if cedar oil can be obtained, it is highly useful as a preservative for the oak.'

'Oak and cypress are abundant in the forests. Cedar, too; we can make the oil.' She turns to Athena. 'Now, the sails. We will need two in case of storm damage. There are looms in the workrooms down here.'

Athena nods, her eyes shining. 'We are all experts with the loom. It will be a pleasure!'

Chryso looks at me. 'Is there anything else?'

'Yes – young fir trees for fifteen-foot oars.'

'We will go scouting tomorrow for all the trees you need.'

'We'll also need water troughs with fresh water to soften the wood for bending. Plus pitch for waterproofing. And lengths of rope for general lashing and the sail.'

Pericles says, 'We can look for many of these things in the storerooms. The wardens seem happy for us to wander around, as long as we stay at this level.'

Chryso nods. 'Good. So, if you and your colleagues can assemble a good supply of saws, I will return tomorrow night, as soon as I have finished my table duties.'

I say quickly, 'If we can take a couple of saws with us now, I can start on the oaks tomorrow.'

And so begins the construction of a vessel that will save lives, not destroy them.

*

I had never thought of Athenians as physically hard workers; from the limited knowledge I picked up through my tutors, they always seemed to be academic types. How wrong I was! From our very first night in the oak woods, these seven young Athenians threw themselves unstintingly into sawing and carrying. I think that the opportunity to use their strong limbs after the confinement of the labyrinth must have come as a wonderful relief. They were cheerful company, too; although they treated me with a deference that I found embarrassing.

Soon, the cave was filling up rapidly with oak and cypress timber stacked against the walls, and I was showing my workforce how to saw the wood into the lengths required for the mortice and tenon construction of the hull. We had built some wooden troughs for the wood softening and brought fresh water from a nearby stream to treat the wood in the hot sun. At this point, too, it was time to give the team a clear idea of what it was they were building; so, with a feeling of fateful familiarity, I found myself drawing the shape of the hull in the sand, lit by the blazing torches. This was also the stage where I had to ask Chryso a potentially sensitive question. 'Is Petra to come with us, my lady? I can make provision for her if you wish.'

She shakes her head with a smile. 'She will not want to leave her home. She is a breed native to Crete only, so it is better if she remains with her wild horse friends in the mountains.'

I say, with a touch of shyness, as I know so little about horses, 'We have some fine Thessalians in Sparta…'

And now Chryso's smile bubbles into a laugh. 'Damian, never mind about me! I will be very happy in Sparta.' Then she adds quietly, 'Especially if you are there.'

Taken aback, I mumble, 'Oh, I'll be there, my lady…' And curse myself afterwards for the total lack of eloquence that goes with being Spartan.

*

As days and nights turn into weeks, the hull begins to take shape on the cave floor. Pericles reports that the girls are weaving a sail of extraordinary beauty and great strength. The Athenians are now adept at finding their way out of the labyrinth and slipping through the patrols, so they no longer need Chryso to guide them. But Chryso herself is causing me some concern. She is as solicitous as ever in looking after the young men and ensuring that they have plenty to drink and eat while they work. But she seems preoccupied, and the sunny smiles come less often.

One night, as everyone is taking a break, sitting on the cave floor, I say quietly to her, 'Has the king said something to you?'

'In a way, that is what worries me. He has said nothing. And yet, when I am waiting at table, he watches me all the time. It makes my skin crawl!'

'Has his wife's attitude to you changed?'

'She was always cold and haughty, so little change there. But while he watches me, she watches him.'

A rumble from the sea vibrates through the cave. Having realised that it is definitely not the Minotaur, the Athenians have become used to it, joking that it must be Poseidon with indigestion – a fancy that I quite like. But I don't like what Chryso is telling me. I jump to my feet. 'Onwards, my friends! And while we work, consider what we should call this ship of ours.'

*

I had become accustomed to snatching a few hours of sleep once my shipbuilding crew had set off to return to the labyrinth. I expect that when they got back, they did the same. I hope Chryso slept for a few hours, too; she would always arrive at the cave just as I was waking. This time, as I open my eyes, her slender silhouette is standing at the mouth of the cave, looking out to sea. Scrambling up and hurrying to her side, I see that she is watching the dark plume of smoke which is once more rising from the horizon. As I reach her, I realise that she is also looking at a sail.

It is not a sail the colour of a pale blood stain, like that of King Odysseus and Pyrrhos. It is a black sail, signifying mourning. Beside me, Chryso is trembling very slightly at the horrors of what happened when she was just eight years old. She whispers, 'It is Orestes. He has come to fetch me home.'

I put an arm around her. 'He is wasting his time. Let's send him on his way.'

Together we walk onto the beach. The black sail is growing larger, the onshore wind carrying them closer. We watch as the crew reef the sail for a controlled beaching. And now we can see the young man standing at the prow. He has shoulder-length dark hair that the wind whips around his face. His complexion is pale, that of a student who spends little time in the sun. The jut of his chin and the heaviness of his brow are reminiscent of the stern features of his father. He looks not in the slightest like his beautiful, golden-haired sister.

As ten or so crew members jump into the water and pull the ship part way onto the sand, Orestes remains standing at the prow. I hug Chryso more closely to my side. Orestes calls to her; the voice is hard, trying to be authoritative. 'Get into the ship, sister!'

I reply, 'She's not going anywhere. But you are.'

Ignoring me, he calls again: 'It is your sacred duty to return and hold our mother to account!'

I retort, 'She has no more duty to any member of her family, dead or alive. Now be on your way!'

He shouts to the crew members on the beach, 'Seize her, you dolts!'

They are a ragged bunch, armed only with daggers. In the split second that they hesitate, I stoop and pick up an axe that we had been using the night before. I have a good aim. It whistles neatly just over the men's heads and embeds itself in the hull of the ship. Having thrown themselves to the ground, thinking that the weapon had been aimed at them, the men struggle to their knees. I advance slowly and steadily towards them. 'Drop your knives!' One by one, they cast their weapons onto the sand. Orestes is by now screaming at them like a demented infant.

Picking up their knives and tucking them into my belt, I say to them, 'Now go. Or I shall enjoy some knife-throwing even more than the axe!'

Ignoring the tantrums of their would-be commander, the men rush to push the ship back into the sea. A task where, being on a lee shore, their colleagues have to disembark and help them. Chryso and I watch as the oarsmen manage to turn the bireme into the waves, the axe protruding grotesquely from its prow. I do not take my eyes off them as the ship becomes smaller. That dark column of smoke is still rising to the clouds as the vessel disappears. Another prolonged rumble plays them out like a drum roll.

Chryso turns to face me and holds my face gently in her hands. Then, she kisses me on the lips with a lingering tenderness.

*

Later that morning, as we walk hand in hand along the beach, I say to her, 'King Idomeneo must have sent for Orestes; he could not otherwise have known of your whereabouts. You must not go back to the palace.'

She says reflectively, 'No. I shall feel far safer in the cave.'

'The shipbuilders can bring bread from their supplies, and there is plenty of fresh water nearby.' I add, with another touch of shyness, 'And I have been trying my hand at fishing during the day.'

She smiles. 'You must teach me. Although I shall always congratulate myself on landing a merman!' Her arms go round me as she kisses me again.

FOUR
ELECTRA

The rumbling, or Poseidon's indigestion as the Athenians put it, usually lasts for a maximum of a few minutes. But one night, while we are all working hard on the growing outer shell of the ship, it does not stop. Hours later, the air is still vibrating around us as the tired shipbuilders prepare to return to the labyrinth. No one says anything, but everyone is on edge.

Early the next morning, the rumbling has at last ceased, although a thick column of smoke now reaches to the clouds. Chryso is still sleeping on the bed of animal skins, while I sleep nearer the entrance to be on the alert for any intruder. All is quiet, as I slip out of the cave and take a brisk jog along the beach. Just before reaching the palace, I divert down a cliff path I have found that will take me, via a short swim, some of it underwater, into Knossos port.

The port is vast; Crete is a mighty sea power. Along the port sides are hundreds of sloping sheds protecting warships from the elements. At anchor, or coming and going, laden with merchandise, are many trading vessels. Even at first light, the place is bustling. Swimming largely underwater to avoid being spotted by the guards, I make my way to a quieter corner of the port where a huddle of fishing boats lies at anchor. Then I see what I have been looking for. A little boat that has seen better times is lying on the dockside; she is covered in barnacles and some of her planks are rotting, but her oars are intact, and she looks just about seaworthy for the distance I have in mind. A quick prowl around and I find the other item I am looking for; a sail is draped over the harbour wall, waiting for a repair to a rip in her centre. Bundling the sail under my arm, I pull the little boat into the water. Five minutes later, I am rowing her out of the port and heading for the beach and the cave.

Chryso is standing on the shore as though she knows exactly what I have been up to. She seems to know me better than I know myself, which I like very much. 'You are going to look for Poseidon's bellyache, aren't you?'

'Once I have made her seaworthy and fitted her with a mast.' I pass the roll of sail to her. 'When we see Pericles tonight, I will ask him to get the girls to repair the rip.'

She shakes out the sail and surveys the tear. 'No need to divert them from the ship's sails. I can mend this and cut it to size to fit our little flying fish here.'

'Is that to be her name?'

'Yes – I am already very fond of her! And how about flying horse for our ship – *Pegasus*!'

'Perfect!'

That night, as work continues on the ship, I show Pericles my latest project. His dark eyes are bright with understanding. 'We know that there is some kind of monster over the far horizon. You are brave to seek it out!'

'You are braver than me – I am leaving you in charge of the shipbuilding until we return. It could be some days.'

'The lady Chryso goes with you?'

I shrug. 'She would never allow me to go without her. She might have to save me from drowning for a second time!'

Pericles laughs. 'You will have a sea nymph for a wife, master shipbuilder!'

'She tells me her best catch was landing a merman. Now, is there anything you need to continue with the ship during our absence?'

He smiles and shakes his head. 'You have been a wonderful teacher.'

'And you are all extraordinary students. I did not know that Athenians could be such hard workers!'

'And we had you Spartans labelled simply as quiet killers, not engineers and inventors!'

And so, while the work on our flying ship *Pegasus* continues during the night, Chryso and I devote ourselves to *Flying Fish*. In two days, I have repaired the central longitudinals to create a keel big enough to take a mast. The mast itself has been designed so that it can be pivoted and quickly lowered with the sail in a sudden squall. This will also lower our centre of gravity and create more stability if we are tossed about in the waves.

In all this, Chryso is my tireless helpmate. Thinking back to how strong she must have been to drag me from the waves and pound all that seawater from my lungs, I find it astonishing how much power there is in those slender limbs. As we work, she tells me what she had been doing before she saw her merman in the stormy sea. 'Every day, I would prepare for the time when I might need to flee Crete. I would swim in the sea for longer and longer distances. I would swim underwater with the fishes, too, and push myself to go deeper and for longer. Do you know how deep you were when I found you, merman?'

'I would guess, very deep?'

'Almost to the sea floor.'

'I must have looked a hopeless case. Did you wonder if it was going to be worth trying?'

Her blue eyes flash. 'I would have brought you back from the dead if I had to!'

'I think you did.'

*

Flying Fish is ready for her maiden voyage and plentifully stocked with food and water. Chryso and I are making last-minute preparations, when I see her looking at the horizon, her face pale. I turn, to see the black sails of three warships rapidly approaching. At the prow of the lead ship stands a woman dressed all in black who is clearly sister to Orestes. She has a heavy brow and an iron jaw; dark hair, pulled back severely from the face; and eyes as hard and unblinking as those of a hawk. She remains at the prow as the ships are beached, and two hundred fully armoured warriors take formation before me.

Electra speaks slowly, almost lazily. 'You can try to fight, Spartan, if you wish. I have heard that your breed lacks nothing in bravery. Or should we call it foolishness? Go ahead! I like to be entertained.'

Chryso puts a hand on my arm. 'You must not. You will be killed.' Swiftly and unhesitatingly, she walks to the ship where her sister waits for her. A gang plank is lowered and with a straight back and proud head, she boards the ship. Her sister Iphigenia must have walked like that towards the sacrificial altar.

As the warriors return their ships to the waves, Electra's parting words are like a double-edged sword: 'Think yourself lucky that we choose to leave you here alive, Spartan. We will be having entertainment enough very soon!'

While the three ships sail towards the horizon, I stand motionless. They have probably lost interest in me by now, but they might just want to make sure. So, I have plenty of time to consider the meaning of those words. The more I think about them, the deeper they cut. Electra was not just referring to her intended murder of her mother and her mother's lover. She was telling me that Chryso too is to die.

As soon as the last sail disappears, I push the little boat into the waves and start rowing. Once I am out in the open sea, I can try to tease some wind into the sail. But for now, I am happy to send my rage into my arms and row like a Fury in pursuit. They will be much faster than me while they are manning their oars. However, when the wind veers, as it frequently does in the Aegean, I will be in a better position than them to take advantage of it. When I feel the breeze swing from being directly in my face to my left side, I raise the mast and brace the sail. It flaps then fills, and the little boat puts on a spurt.

How easy it had been to send Orestes and his ragged crew on their way. And how beyond impossible with his iron-jawed sister. I should have foreseen that Electra would not have her purpose defeated. I can imagine how she must have tongue-lashed her brother for returning empty-handed. I feel sorry for Orestes: dragged from his comfortable life as a student in Athens to become an accomplice to matricide and assassination. I feel the same way about Pyrrhos: inheriting the duty of vengeance for the death of a father he never knew, with a reputation that he could never live up to. But I feel a desperate fury at myself for allowing this to happen to Chryso.

The favourable wind is strengthening, and we have a good, fast run for an hour or so. So fast, that at one point I glimpse the tip of a black sail ahead of me and immediately lower the mast and take to my oars. They must be assuming that I would not dream of going after them. Let them continue to think that!

Night falls and the clear sky makes it easy for me to navigate by the pole star. I have seldom been at sea during the hours of darkness. Tonight, the sky is full of meteorites, which fall in sparkling showers over my head. But most wonderful of all is when I look down into a sea of stars, the surface of the water seeming to glow with myriads of tiny, dancing lights. When I row, the sea light flows off the planes of my oars, its enchantment continuing until the dawn.

Glad of the food and drink we stowed, I row on into the Etesian winds all the following day. Thinking of the time when, Chryso at my side again, we will have a following wind and a full sail to return to Crete. And soon after, escape any further vengeful pursuit by sailing with our Athenian friends to my homeland. Chryso understanding me as well as she does, I am certain that she knows I am coming for her. But I dread that I may not reach her in time. This fear fires fresh energy into aching arms and blistered hands, and I redouble my efforts to catch up with the black-sailed ships.

That night brings a storm that roars for hours. The little boat weathers the waves with tenacity, but the cloud cover makes it impossible to navigate and I fear very much that I could be going back the way I have come, or at least round in circles. With the dawn, I at last regain my bearings. Through some incredible stroke of luck or sheer instinct, I have continued on course during the night. Giving hearty thanks to Poseidon, I sense a favourable breeze and decide to hoist the sail while I take some food and drink. The little sail snaps and fills, and we set off at a lively pace, onwards towards the Gulf of Aulis, where lie Mycenae and the mighty palace of Chryso's murdered father, King Agamemnon.

As *Flying Fish* dances across the waves, we are joined by some playful company. A pair of dolphins arc into the air on our port side. They plunge into the sea and reappear to starboard, squeaking with delight. I assume it is delight, as I have never before seen creatures who appear to be so wholeheartedly happy with themselves and the world in general. At one point, they surface right alongside my little boat and peer up at me with their perpetual grin. I cease rowing and smile back at them, convinced that their presence is a good sign for my mission and remembering the wonderfully true-to-life dolphin fresco from long ago that greeted Chryso and me in the labyrinth.

Shortly after the dolphins have departed for fresh playgrounds, I see something that has the opposite effect on my spirits. I have to swerve to avoid a length of ship's mast as it floats past, trailing the ribbons of a black sail. Is this debris from one of the warships of Electra? If they were trying to make way under sail in last night's storm, then it can be no wonder that they capsized and were dismasted. Was there no sailor among them to warn them against such folly?

An hour more of sailing, and the wind drops. But to my joy I can see why. A shore is in sight to the west. Hopefully it is the peninsula of Aulis, where I hope to make landfall. Almost at the same time as I sight the peninsula, I see more mast wreckage, this time with a man clinging to it, looking more dead than alive. It is an unspoken law at sea that you give aid to those who need it. They may be enemy or friend; in the ocean, they are neither. The common bond of humanity makes it imperative to give help if you can.

Drawing alongside him, I ship my oars. He opens red-rimmed, salt-seared eyes and stares at me as though I am the last apparition he will see before descending into Hades. I say, 'Can you manage to get aboard?' He is very weak, but after a struggle, I succeed in pulling him into the boat without capsizing us. He lies exhausted. I pass him a flagon of water, warning, 'Do not drink too fast – it will make you ill!'

As he drinks, I resume my rowing. We are approaching the mouth of the gulf that will take us to Aulis: the fateful setting for the death by sacrifice of Chryso's sister. I pass my passenger some honey bread. He starts to cram it into his mouth, then remembers my warning with a rueful grin and takes a small bite. 'Thank you, my friend. I owe you my life.'

'Were you on one of Princess Electra's ships?'

'With my platoon, yes.'

I have to force the words out. 'Was it the ship that carried her and her sister?'

'No. They had an admiral in charge of their ship. We had a homicidal maniac at our helm.'

'He tried to sail in the storm?'

'With predictable results. I jumped clear as she capsized then turned turtle. My colleagues were trapped in the hull. I fear all are lost.'

'I am sorry.'

He looks at me more closely. 'You are the one-man army we were sent to cut to pieces, aren't you?'

'I am very glad that you let me live.'

'So am I; thanks to you I am alive now. Although I wonder that she did.'

'I think I now understand why. She intends to kill Princess Chrysothemis, and she wants me to know that.'

'And you are trying to stop her. She will not expect that. She is used to getting her own way.'

'Will you be going back to your barracks at Mycenae?'

'To be flogged within an inch of my life for surviving a shipwreck that killed all my brothers-in-arms?' He shakes his head. 'I will go and seek service in Thebes. Many of us have already done so.' He takes another drink of water. 'But first, my friend, I may be able to be of service to you. You will be seeking Princess Chrysothemis at the palace, yes?'

I nod.

'I can tell you about the layout of the palace and how to gain entrance; where she is likely to be held; and an escape route.'

I lean forward and shake his hand. 'Damian.'

'Antiochus. We are well met, Damian.'

At Aulis, Antiochus shows me a place to beach the little boat where she is concealed from thieving eyes. Then we set off on the road to Mycenae. He begins, 'The palace is one of the most heavily fortified anywhere. The walls are more than forty feet high and nearly thirty feet thick, made of stone blocks weighing up to six tonnes. Authorised visitors enter the fortress through the Lion's Gate, the two massive rearing lions being the insignia of the Royal House of Atrius. You, however, must make your way to the north-east walls, where you will find a spring. Beside this spring, a little searching will show you the secret entrance to a vaulted tunnel, which runs beneath the Postern Gate. The tunnel will take you into the servants' quarters. On the floor above are the royal apartments, where the king was murdered and where, no doubt, Prince Orestes and Princess Electra intend to deal the same fate to Queen Clytemnestra and her lover. It is possible that Princess Chrysothemis is in a room adjacent to her mother's. You will soon see, because there will be a guard outside. That same secret tunnel is your escape route with the princess. The barracks are not far from the north-east wall and not guarded. In the stables you will find horses. May the gods guide you, my friend!'

*

Antiochus's description of the palace was apt; its mighty walls remind me of the inner citadel of Troy. It seems an apt twist of fate, too, that the man who led the Greek world against that city now lies in a freshly built and heavily garlanded tomb outside his own palace. Soon after passing the tomb, which stands alone without a single mourner, I find the secret tunnel. It is well built, as Antiochus said, with a generous width and vaulted ceiling. Climbing the stone steps, I wonder if Orestes will be using it to make his escape after the murder of his mother.

The servants' quarters are deserted; below must be the kitchen, with a large banquet presumably being prepared, such is the clamour and clash of pans and dishes. Leaving this humble dormitory, with its rows of straw mattresses, I find a stairway with an embroidered curtain drawn across. On passing through, I mount steps with ornate frescoes adorning the walls: the route to the royal apartments.

On tiptoe, I steal along the corridor and spy the guard that Antiochus told me of. Unseen by him, round a corner, I shout, 'Halt, thief!' He rushes to see what the commotion is; a thump on the head knocks him senseless; and I quickly don his armour and his sword and dagger. That way, I can pretend to be escorting the prisoner for interrogation if I am challenged. Outside her door, I whisper, 'Flying Fish!' and gently push it open. Chryso has been tied to a chair and gagged, but her blue eyes flash me a greeting. Quickly, I free her, and we run from that room, along the corridor, past the inert body of the guard and down the stairs to the servants' quarters.

Everything is going perfectly until I pick the wrong door for the tunnel entrance, and we find ourselves at the back of a musicians' gallery, looking directly down at the scene of the banquet. Frozen, we can see Orestes and Electra sitting either side of a couple who must be Queen Clytemnestra and her paramour. Maybe fifty guests are chatting, laughing, eating and drinking at the banqueting tables. The queen herself – a stern-looking but handsome woman of middle age – is listening to something that her lover is whispering in her ear, a slight smile on her face. Electra, robed for once not in black but in brocaded gold silk, is looking fixedly at her mother, her face wooden. Orestes is making small talk with the older man at his side; he looks as though he would rather be anywhere but here. Then a sudden loud burst of laughter breaks our paralysis; we melt back into the corridor, and I pick the right door into the tunnel.

That scene will return to haunt me for years. I felt like a ghost, looking down on the two people who were soon to die, with the precious being next to me who would have joined them in death if the killers had succeeded. In silence, we hurry down the stone steps; then we are out in the fresh air and away from the stench of murder. I whisper, 'Can you lead us to the barracks? I am informed that we can find horses there.'

She nods and takes my hand. Hers is warm, closing around mine with her firm grip. The gate to the barracks is open; the place looks deserted. The stable yard is round the back. Chryso seems to have been here before and I remember her skill as a rider; perhaps she used to ride the army horses. She goes quickly down the stalls and picks a chestnut mare for herself and a sturdy brown gelding for me. The animals are soon saddled and bridled; in minutes we are galloping away, down the road that will take us to Aulis and our little boat.

After we have left the palace far behind, Chryso slows the pace to a trot – which nearly unseats me – and then, mercifully, a walk. 'We do not want to tire them. Besides, I do not fear pursuit just yet.'

With a cold feeling, I ask her, 'Why is that?'

'It is Orestes who will be pursued. They are planning to kill our mother the queen and her lover tonight. Electra thinks she will be able to pin the blame on one or more of the guests. It won't work. But Electra will make sure that her brother, not her, is named as the culprit.'

She is silent and I fill in the words she has not said. 'She was planning to kill you too, wasn't she?'

She nods, and the Furies howl in my head once more. Despite the fact that I have freed Chryso, I still feel that both of us are trapped inside a story that some demonic force has created. At any time, just when we are tasting the sweetness of success, everything will go horribly wrong. All through the rest of that ride to Aulis, I am haunted by the nightmares that I had at Troy, when we were pinned on the beaches by the perfidious winds. Suppose we are met by the same conditions when we get to the gulf?

FIVE

FIRE AND WATER

To my great relief, there is barely the hint of a breeze when we arrive at Aulis, and the little boat is where I left it. Tying up the horses at a trough where they can drink and rest, we launch *Flying Fish* into the water. Chryso insists on taking an oar, and side by side we row through the gulf and towards the sea. As we enter open water, the breeze starts to pick up; once we are out in the ocean, we will have the Etesians blowing us back to Crete. It is just before dawn; the dark spectres of my night-time fears are fading. Tinges of pink and grey are starting to streak the horizon, when I say to Chryso, 'You must eat and drink now. You have had nothing for far too long!'

She does as I tell her, taking long draughts of the water and eating the honey bread, while I row onwards towards the Aegean. I watch her as she eats and drinks, feeling a kind of terror at the narrow margin of time left to us when I found her. I tell her of the soldier I rescued and how he gave me such invaluable advice. She smiles. 'You were of great help to each other. You both deserved it!'

Then we are silent as I bend to the oars. Each thinking of the terrible events that have probably by now taken place. As though vengeance, a death for a death, can ever make anything right, instead of infinitely worse. Seeming to read my mind, Chryso says softly, 'Do you know what my name means, merman?'

'Your full name – Chrysothemis: The Golden Way? It's a term we sometimes use in shipbuilding to get a line perfectly balanced and straight.'

She smiles again. 'I love that you use it to build perfect ships! But The Golden Way also means what you must not do if you want to live a good life. You must not do what you would blame others for doing.'

I ponder this. 'Do you think Electra would blame someone for murdering their mother?'

She reflects on this question, watching the rise and fall of my oars and the water drops flashing in the rising sun. 'I take your point. I find it difficult to think that she would.'

'And yet, you tell me that she will try and make Orestes take all the blame. In trying to avoid blame, she must know that what she has done is wrong.'

Chryso's blue eyes blaze. 'She must know, yes. But you saw when she came for me how much she enjoys the act of killing as an "entertainment". When Electra put on mourning, it wasn't grief for her sister. She was already looking forward to what she knew would happen to her father. An act that would, to her, justify her murder of her mother.'

'Do you think it does justify that?'

Chryso comes across to sit next to me and takes her oar back. We pull vigorously as she says, 'Never! She should have brought my mother and Aegisthus to justice and let the courts decide.'

'I think I can work out why she would want Orestes to take the blame. In Athens, and probably many other Greek states, they would consult the oracle. And the oracle would say that the gods commanded Orestes as the son to take vengeance. That's bound to get him off, isn't it?'

'That's doubtless what my sister would want the oracle to say. But would it have any credibility in Sparta?'

'We don't pay such slavish attention to the gods as the rest of the Greek world. Not when it comes to murder, anyway. In Sparta, the rule of law is more powerful than the sword. And maybe the gods, too.'

*

Despite what Chryso said about not expecting to be pursued just yet, I keep a close eye on the waters behind us. Having been taken once horribly by surprise, I do not intend it to happen again. So, as we leave the gulf and head into the Aegean, we flit from the shelter of one island to another. If we see a hint of pursuit, we can lower the mast in a flash.

The Etesians now provide us with a following wind that *Flying Fish* runs before at a good pace. Chryso laughs with delight. 'She's well named, isn't she?' As if welcoming us back, two dolphins now leap and plunge gracefully alongside our little boat. Chryso tells me, 'When I was working at my swimming, I would sometimes play with these beautiful creatures!' As they approach with their cheerful smiles, she leans over to lightly stroke their heads and is rewarded with a shower of squeaks and squeals. I tell her about the dolphins that accompanied me to Aulis; she exclaims, 'I'm sure they are the same ones!'

At night, when the winds drop, we take it in turns to sleep while the other rows. Comes the dawn and the winds wake again, pushing us ever southwards and ever further away from the gloomy, bloody palace of Mycenae. On one clear night, Chryso wakes to see the tiny luminous stars that run in rivers from the tips of my oars. She dips a hand into the luminescence, her golden hair trailing in the water; and no sea nymph in any ocean in the world could ever be as beautiful as she is.

As the sun sinks in the west the following day, I see puffy black clouds massing on the horizon. We are not far from one of the many small islands of the Cyclades, and I come to a decision. 'I don't want to chance our luck in riding this one out. Let's take cover!' Pulling the little boat well onto the beach, we find shelter in a small cave and are treated to a night of heavenly histrionics. The winds, instead of dropping towards evening in the usual fashion of the Etesians, rise to a gale that whips the waves into a fury. Booming thunder accompanies sheet lightning that illuminates the sea with a lurid purple. And the temperature drops alarmingly, to a point where I hold Chryso close to warm her.

In the morning the hot sun returns, and with it comes a visitor. As we peer out of the cave, munching on some honey bread, a large, oval shell starts to appear from the waves and, above it, a scaly, beaked head. I have seen turtles before but never this big. She trundles up the beach and starts to dig. These are going to be some of the deepest-buried eggs anywhere; she is still digging as we launch *Flying Fish* and take our leave.

Sailing on southwards with the Etesians filling our little sail, we see the ominous sign of pieces of masts and oars floating in the water. I say, 'It could have been last night's storm claiming a new victim. But it could also be the warship that went down with all souls lost but Antiochus.'

The following day, Chryso points to a familiar dark plume of smoke on the horizon to the south of us. 'That is Poseidon's bellyache, isn't it?'

'Do you still want to see what it is?'

'Yes. We need to know. That sound is no Minotaur!'

By the time we reach the black island with its conical dark mountain, the smoke has gone. The wind drops completely, and we row in a flat calm towards the beach. The sea has a strange, pale-blue glow which is nothing like the sparkling luminescence we saw during the night. Pulling the little boat onto the shore, we can feel heat radiating from the sand. We are wearing sandals; it would be unbearable for naked feet. We pause and look upwards. Still no smoke and no rumbles. The beast is slumbering. Only, the sky above us is not the clear, bright blue that it was. It is as though some kind of haze is between us and the heavens.

Chryso grasps my hand. 'Come on!' We start to climb. As soon as we leave the beach, the air on the mountain becomes foetid and heavy with smoke. We cannot see the smoke, but we cannot help breathing it either. Soon, we are both coughing, and our eyes are streaming. Chryso gasps. 'This place is poisonous!'

'Shall we get out now?'

'We can't waste our one chance to find out!'

So, we press on upwards. The slope is gradual, but the air becomes ever thicker with the invisible toxic fumes. We are within a hundred yards of the summit, when the first rumble shakes the ground beneath our feet. A thin plume of smoke coils upwards, then subsides. We struggle onwards. A jagged rim about two hundred feet wide waits above us. We are within fifty feet of the rim, when a second powerful shaking pushes us to the scorching ground, burning our hands and knees. Scrambling up, hands over our mouths, we make a final bid for the rim. Met by a massive blast of heat, we stare down into Hades.

I did not know that rock could melt and become a river of fire. Below us is a vast cauldron of melting, boiling, churning, writhing liquid rock. The heat is so searing that we can only take the briefest of glimpses before turning and scrambling for our lives back down the slope. The mountain shakes once more, and again we are thrown to our knees in burning black sand. I take Chryso's arm, and we stumble on downwards. Then, with a mighty roar, the fire mountain sends an unending thick, black cloud skywards. Glowing ash falls like red-hot needles on our skin. We get to the beach, push our little boat into the waves and row as though demented. The smoke column now reaches to the clouds and day is turning to night.

As we flee from the fire mountain, rivers of melted rock stream down the slopes and hit the seawater with cataclysmic explosions. The sea is bubbling around us, and our throats are burning with the fumes. I am fearful that the fiery ash raining down on us could cause our little boat to catch fire. And still this awful calm continues. No sign of the Etesians that we need to blow us to Crete. The sky is dark, the black cloud from the fire mountain covering us like a shroud. And I start to wonder if this is the ending we were always heading for, the one that was written for us from the beginning.

So, I don't dare to hope when there comes a whisper of a wind. Perhaps it is simply the Furies playing with us; we are their entertainment. But the whisper persists; it becomes a slight breeze. The breeze does not die; it strengthens. I put a hand on Chryso's arm to tell her to take a rest from rowing, and I hoist the sail. It wavers, then snaps and tightens. *Flying Fish* lifts her prow into the waves and dances on the water.

I don't know how long it took us to get back to Crete. The daytime night created by the black cloud from the fire mountain lasted for the entire voyage. And I still did not permit myself to hope, because even when our feet were on Cretan sand, I told myself, the Furies could still make disaster strike. In fact, it strikes minutes before we make landfall. It is many hours since we left the roaring of the fire mountain behind; we have been lulled into a sense of security by the steady buffeting of the wind. It is a false sense of security. Because now, with the Crete shore just yards away, we are shaken by a thunder that seems to come from the depths of the ocean itself.

Lowering the sail, I jump into the sea and pull our boat onto the shore as Pericles runs towards us from the direction of the cave. He stares, horrified, at our burns. Then, he looks towards the sea, and his face changes again. We turn. In an eerie quietness, the waters are retreating: inexorably receding from the beach, as though a giant force is sucking them towards the horizon. Whole expanses of golden sand now lie naked, with wracks of seaweed and seashells abandoned in the wastes, while the waters disappear across the horizon.

I say urgently, 'I have seen this once before, on Skyros. A great wave will come. We must climb. Go and warn your men, Pericles!'

He doesn't move. 'The labyrinth! We have to save the women!'

'The palace and the labyrinth are far higher up than we are. And we can never get there in time to help. We must save ourselves if we want to save them!'

The logic of my words strikes home, and we all three run to the cave. His colleagues have been standing outside, staring at the retreating tide and the empty expanses that are left; they are all too willing to follow us up the cliffs. We have scrambled to a height of maybe a hundred feet, when we hear a faint roar, gathering in intensity. Across the entire far horizon, a thin, silver ribbon rapidly turns into a vast wave travelling at a terrifying speed towards us. The roaring now fills the sky, and the wave is rushing towards us at a height of seventy feet or more. It smashes into the cliff and drenches us with spray, but our perch is high enough to keep us out of harm's way. I can picture what must be happening down on the beach, with the wave hurtling onwards and into the forest, downing trees and everything else in its path.

For an hour or more the angry waters swirl and froth

just below us, and we have no choice but to wait until they go down. The cliff is too steep to climb any further upwards and try for a route along the top. As soon as the tide drops to a few feet deep, we swarm back down the cliff and the Athenians set off at a run for the labyrinth. Chryso and I wade into the cave to see what damage has been done to our ship. She has been picked up and dashed against the cave walls, but her longitudinal members have held up well. I take a look inside the hull. 'We can soon repair this. But we must get her out of here, round to the western side of the island.'

'You think there will be another wave?'

'When I was on Skyros, there was just the one. But this is not Skyros!'

We start to make our way towards the labyrinth. When we come to the place where we beached *Flying Fish*, there is no sign of the little boat. The forest beyond is a wreckage of fallen trees. Chryso says, 'I suppose she could have been smashed to pieces.'

'I'm afraid it's quite likely. But she has served us well!'

We press on, and the high walls of the palace loom into view. Conscious that we normally only enter the labyrinth at night, I am wary of the guards. But everywhere is quiet; even the birdsong has been silenced by the trauma of the wave. I whisper, 'I think that all of Idomeneo's soldiers must be down at the port. This must have dealt his naval and trading fleets a heavy blow.'

We flit through the entrance to the labyrinth and downwards, relieved to see that there is no evidence of any seawater having entered. The girls have heard nothing of the cataclysm and have been quietly getting on with their work on the sails, which look to be almost complete. Pericles says to me, 'Is our ship damaged?'

'Nothing that cannot be quickly repaired. But we must now adapt our plans in the light of what has happened.'

Pericles' dark eyes hold mine. 'You think that there will be another wave, don't you, my friend? Possibly an even bigger one?'

'We must act as though we believe that to be the case. If there is a second wave – or even a third – it could flood the labyrinth. We must all travel to a place of safety on the western side of the island. The ship must be moved there too.' I add, watching their eyes brighten, 'From the western shore, we will be in an ideal position to sail for Sparta!'

Pericles says, 'There has been no sign of the wardens. They are probably down at the docks, trying to deal with the damage.'

'So now is the right time to make a start. We need to pack all the provisions we can for the journey to the west.'

Chryso agrees: 'I can find some pack animals in the palace stables. Carts as well. And that is where they store flour, olives and figs.'

'I will come with you. Electra and Orestes could be in league with Idomeneo; he must not know that you are here.'

Pericles looks in concern at our arms. 'How are you both so burned? You look as though you have been through fire as well as water!'

Chryso answers him. 'We have been to the mountain that was sending out the plumes of smoke. We were lucky to escape with our lives!'

I add, 'But I'm not so sure that the wave came from the fire mountain. There was a deep thundering from beneath the ocean shortly before we landed at Crete; it was after that sound that the wave came.'

Pericles looks at me. 'Was it like that at Skyros?'

'Exactly like that.'

'Either way, it does not matter, does it? We need to get out of here. And, as you say, my friend, now is the best possible time!'

The rest of that day, we all busy ourselves packing for the trek to the western shore. It is a journey of more than one hundred miles overland and more by sea. I feel confident that we are all in good shape for it. Chryso whispers to me that two of the Athenian wives are in the early stages of pregnancy but feeling very well. As Pericles said, all the wardens must be down at the port, as there is no sign of them during the entire time that we pack. Having accompanied Chryso to the stables to collect provisions, pack animals and carts without meeting a soul, I wonder what awful inundation has hit the port of Knossos. I also have a lingering hope that I might find something we have lost. So, I make my way to the port by my old route, swimming sometimes underwater, to avoid detection by King Idomeneo's soldiers.

They are trying to tidy up a battlefield, as though an enemy fleet had sailed unchallenged into Knossos port and rammed every ship on the water. Soldiers are beaching wrecks, piling them on the shore and setting fire to them like giant funeral pyres. The air is full of smoke, although nothing like as noxious as the toxic fumes on the fire mountain. The only ships that seem to have survived the havoc are the hundred or so warships in the sheds, and they cannot have avoided some damage. No wonder that the labyrinth is empty of guards. Crete's supremacy as a great sea power, a thalassocracy, has never before been dealt such a blow. And will there be a yet greater disaster? Will the wave return, even higher than before?

While I am swimming out of the port, I see an old friend. High and dry on the deck of a wrecked trading ship, tossed there by the wave and miraculously intact, is *Flying Fish*. As I scramble up to her, some of the men from the pyres are approaching to beach and torch the wreck. Quickly, I drag the little craft to the edge of the sloping deck, slide her in and dive in after her. Behind me, the wrecked ship is soon going up in flames. I have no oars, so I hand paddle around the docks, until I can find ones that will do from among all the floating debris. Even the sail and its pivot are intact. This is good news. It means that, regardless of the state of our ship, we can tow her to the western shore if necessary. Feeling triumphant, I row our little boat to the cave, where preparations are well underway for our departure.

Chryso is ecstatic to have *Flying Fish* back. She says, 'Everything is ready for the overland route. As soon as *Pegasus* is launched, we can load the provisions for the voyage.'

The Athenians have by this time completely evacuated the labyrinth. With Pericles and four of his colleagues, we pull the nearly complete hull of *Pegasus* out of the cave and into the sea. She is a neat little ship with two single rows of oars, seven to a side, with room fore and aft for provisions. I have designed her with a deeper keel than a bireme, because she is small enough to pull onto the shore whilst having a lower centre of gravity, which will help us in storms. The mast is complete but yet to be fitted; it will travel lying in the centre of the ship, with the sails stowed aft. The rudder too, consisting of two oars to be attached to the stern and controlled by ropes, will be fitted when we get to the safety of the western shore. The damage that she has sustained is above her waterline so should not pose a risk.

Finally, all is set. *Pegasus* is successfully launched and the supplies loaded. Pericles and three of his comrades are aboard, with an oar apiece. The three other men are travelling with the women overland, and they are already on their way with their carts, provisions and pack animals. I have forewarned the oarsmen that *Pegasus* will take on water while the wood swells to form a tight seal; it should not be long before the water ingress slows and then stops. Chryso and I launch *Flying Fish* and scramble aboard; Pericles throws us the towing line, which we fasten to our stern. As we leave the black sand and begin the voyage westwards, the smoke column is dispersing and the fire mountain is silent. How long the monster will remain like that is anybody's guess.

We have many days of travel before we can reach the western shore. Most of that time, if there is another great wave, we will be directly in its path. Our land travellers are safe, on mountain tracks that will take them higher than any wave can rise.

I wonder if King Idomeneo has noticed the departure of the couples who were to boost the population of Crete. I doubt it. He must have many other things on his mind. He may have learned of the murder of the wife of his former comrade-in-arms by Electra and Orestes; he may even have connived at it, by betraying Chryso's whereabouts to them. But foremost in his thoughts must be how vulnerable Crete is now, with her navy half-destroyed and the remains of her trading fleet on fire in Knossos port. He knows that Mycenae has been envious of Crete's power for many years.

SIX

WIND AND WAVE

It is far from easy for a small boat to tow a much larger ship through the lively waters of the Aegean. After a few scares, when the ship comes close to crashing into our stern, we lengthen the tow line to keep a safer distance between us. Then, there is the question of who is towing who. If a large wave turns the prow of the ship suddenly out to sea, our little boat gets dragged that way too. The best we can provide – when we can – is directional stability, because without a rudder, the ship is unsteerable.

We have agreed in advance with Pericles that, in the event of bad weather, we will instantly make for the beach and find whatever shelter we can. Inevitably, it isn't long before the Etesians start to gain in strength. Glancing at the shore, I can see a line of treacherous rocks that we must negotiate if we choose to make landfall here. Many of the rocks could also be unseen, just below the water. I signal to Pericles that we must press on, pointing to the rocks.

As conditions worsen, the Etesians are now pushing us hard onshore, and our little boat is having to be turned with its prow pointing seawards to try and counter this. Very soon, such a tactic will not be sustainable. We are now past the rocks that can be seen. Coming to a decision, I attach a tow line to the prow of our little boat, wrap it round my waist, jump into the water and swim towards the shore. A bit like a human pilot ship; if anyone is going to find rocks, I and not our ships' hulls, will be the first. As soon as my feet touch the sand, I wave to the Athenians, and they leap into the waves and guide the ship safely to the beach. Chryso follows, and we all make landfall unscathed, having developed a highly useful plan for dealing with rocks. Although, if the wind force had been any greater, I doubt if I could have prevented our vessels from being driven helplessly ashore in a totally uncontrolled beaching.

We sheltered on that beach for the night, huddled beside the boats, while the winds howled relentlessly from dark to dawn. In the morning, while we wait for the waves to settle, I try my hand at fishing off a rocky outcrop and am rewarded by a substantial catch of grey mullet. Roasted over a fire, the fish meal puts everyone in a good mood; the onshore wind having now dropped, we set off again on our westwards sea trek.

We are about two hours into this next leg, when Chryso touches my arm and points to the horizon. With a cold feeling, I see the column of smoke snaking skywards once more. The storm has dispersed the ash clouds, but the fire mountain is now wide awake again. Pericles and his men have seen it too. We buckle down to our rowing to increase the distance between us and the inferno. As though reminding us that we are nowhere near the safe shores that we are seeking, a familiar rumbling travels across the waters to us; it continues at intervals as regular as when I first landed on the black sand of Crete.

I look at Chryso; the burn marks on her arms are quickly healing, after she found olive oil among our supplies and insisted on applying it to my skin too. Her powers of endurance never cease to amaze me. For a teenage girl as slight as a sea nymph, she has the strength of a goddess. As though sensing my gaze, she looks at me, leans towards me and kisses me full on the lips. 'You look in your element, merman.'

'Only because I am with you, my lady.'

*

The onshore Etesian winds blew more gently all that day and, as they were wont to do, dropped completely towards evening. So, we took full advantage and rowed steadily onwards through the night, the seas lit by a glorious full moon and that magical luminescence.

By dawn the next day, the rugged coastline that we have been hugging has turned into a broad, sheltered bay, many miles in length. The promontory that we have passed extends far out into the sea behind us. From my limited knowledge of the island of Crete, I have to guess that we could now be well over halfway to the western shore. And I am grateful that we have this promontory to protect us. Because the seas are trembling again with mighty thunderings in their depths.

I signal to Pericles that we must continue to press on through the night. And all through that night, lit by an intermittent moon from trailing clouds, the undersea roaring grows in strength. In the dark, I can't see if the fire mountain is still smoking. But it sounds as though below us the seabed is in turmoil. And I am becoming more and more convinced that the mountain and the wave are not directly linked. Now, my feeling is that there could be another wave before anything else happens. The more we can pull ourselves into the shelter of this vast bay, the safer we will be. For four days we row, while the thundering ocean tosses restlessly. The entire bay is beginning to churn with boiling water, when I signal that we have to head for the shore.

We have beached when the blast comes and the sand shudders beneath our feet. Within twenty seconds, the tide starts to recede, leaving behind miles of naked sand. We pull the boats as far up the beach as we can and lash them down to try and stop them from being torn away by the returning water. Then, we stare at the empty horizon, listening. A faint roaring tells us that the wave is on its way. And this time, to our horror, the thin ribbon on the horizon turns into a wall of water that is easily twice as big as the previous wave; this monster looks to be more than 150 feet high. I have gambled everything on the hope that the promontory will funnel the main force of the wave towards the northern shores of the island. And to my enormous relief, that is what happens. By some gift of the gods, we have been saved. Large waves crash onto the shore and lift our boats from the sand. Heavy tides swirl around us for days and nights. But we are all alive and our precious craft undamaged. I fear that few in the palace of Knossos, the labyrinth and the port will have fared as well as we have.

*

I will not pretend that it suddenly became easier to reach the western shore after we survived the second great wave. The winds were as bullying as ever, shoving us onshore and making us fight to keep going. We had to endure three more storms, finding whatever shelter we could, on beaches where the fishing was so poor that our supplies were starting to run low.

But one bright morning, Chryso and I find ourselves rowing round a headland and taking a definitive turn to the south. We have reached the western shore and, suddenly, the Etesians are in our favour again. With a full sail, *Flying Fish* is now really towing *Pegasus*, while the Athenians cheer and row hard to speed us onwards. And now we have to find the land party and rejoin forces, assuming that they have reached the destination before us, which is anything but certain. We might have had giant waves and storms to contend with, but they could have been up against robber bands, wild animals and difficult territory. The more I consider these factors, the more concerned I become and the more certain that I have sent these travellers into grave danger.

Chryso says, 'We must hug the shore. They could be anywhere!'

'Pericles says they will be flying a flag – the spare sail from *Pegasus*.'

But the further we go along the western coast, the more convinced we are that we are the first arrivals. Increasingly, the worry gnaws at me about the misfortunes that could have befallen the little band of three men, seven women and their pack animals and carts. As a seafarer, I am woefully ignorant of the land routes of Crete, and ignorance and peril are all too often fellow travellers. Over the next few days, we sail the entire length of the western shore and see no sign of our friends. So, we turn and beat against the Etesians until we see a small inlet with a cave opening onto the beach. We drag the little boat and the ship ashore. And find the Athenians camped within the cave, exhausted and starving.

They had no means of defence against the robber band that swooped on them two days into the journey and took their pack animals and supplies. Amid great hardship, they had to forage off the land to make the long journey to the western coast. I curse myself for not thinking carefully enough about the risks they were to run. For not trying to better arm the three Athenian men; maybe I could have raided the wreckage in the port for weapons. I burn with shame at having sent these vulnerable Athenians into such appalling danger. They could so easily all have been killed. All that I had thought of was their safety from another great wave; I had barely at all considered what perils I was sending them into.

We give them all the food and water we have left. Then Pericles and I take a bow and arrow each into the mountains. We return with two wild goats, light a fire and roast the meat until the evening sizzles with the mouth-watering odour. That night, everyone feasts until they can eat no more. And I feel my anger and self-reproach turning into a kind of joy that everyone has made this journey. We are reunited, and now we all have but one purpose.

*

The following morning, Pericles goes off with two of his men to hunt for more meat, while I lead the working party to repair *Pegasus* and fit the rudder and the mast. We have brought all the tools we need; around us there are trees enough to patch up the ship and make her seaworthy for the voyage to Sparta. The spare sail was stolen by the robbers on the land journey, but we have a beautiful and very serviceable sail that we stowed on the ship; pure white, she has an embroidered flying horse motif.

We eat well as we prepare for the maiden voyage of *Pegasus*. Pericles and his men have developed a taste for hunting, and the wild mountain goats make good eating. We find everything we need to make replacement timbers for the damaged hull, and soon she is as good as new. Then we put *Pegasus* to sea to test the rudder and the mast. On this western shore, the winds are gentle, and it is easy to steady her as I make a few final adjustments. The fitted sail billows in the breeze. And we gaze in satisfaction at our beautiful little ship.

Seeing those puffy, black clouds on the horizon again, we reef the sail and drag the ship as far up the beach as we can, lashing her tightly. With the mast fitted, she is more top-heavy and likely to tip over. Pericles says, 'What do you think of the weather for tomorrow?'

My reply is drowned by a thunderclap louder than I have ever heard before. On the horizon, sheet lightning illuminates the sea and sky like the anger of Zeus. A vast, dark cloud shot with leaping red flames mushrooms quickly upwards. The fire mountain is blowing itself to pieces.

The previous eruption was like a child playing games; this one looks like the end of all things. If a third wave follows, it could be the end of all things for Idomeneo's kingdom.

*

Having snatched a few hours' sleep, we all rise while the dark continues and launch the boats by torchlight. Loading the remaining provisions, we then see to the arrangement of the crew. Alternating Athenian men and women to spread the balance of strength as evenly as possible, we set up a rowing shift system for the women, with hourly rest periods and a seat at the stern as lookout. Pericles' wife Athena takes that place first. With *Flying Fish* attached by a tow rope to the stern, we push *Pegasus* further into the small waves and scramble aboard. A favourable breeze blows on our beam, as we set sail for Sparta.

For the first day, I am kept fully occupied training the crew to row. Even with just a single bank of oars, unlike a bireme, it takes time to learn how to synchronise the strokes so that the oars move as one. Then the women come up with a chant that perfectly fits with the cycle of the oar dipping, pulling and rising, and the men cheerfully join in. From the giggles of the wives, I guess that some of the Athenian men are improvising on the chant to create cheeky sea shanties.

It barely seems to get light at all that day; towards what must be evening, we beach on a small island which, I know from experience, has fresh water and good fishing. The land travellers are all now fully recovered from their ordeal, and the resilience of the women in particular deeply impresses me, but I still reflect with shame on my failure of leadership in causing them to be exposed to such danger and hardship. And yet they show no trace of resentment at what I have put them through. Truly, these Athenians are a remarkable people whom it is a privilege to know.

*

My fishing skills are improving, even in the dark, where there are actually more fish visiting my bait. With campfires burning and the fish roasting with herbs, we make an excellent meal of it. It is suffocatingly warm, but I suggest that everyone sleeps within the shelter of the small caves looking onto the beach; I can sense a storm coming, and Pericles and I lash the boats tightly. The wind blows hard all night; in the early hours, there are faint signs of dawn in the east, and that second day of the voyage to Sparta is slightly less dark than the first one. After taking food and water, we set off on the next leg of the journey.

Bending strongly to her oar, Chryso says, 'You know these seas well, merman.'

'I had never actually been to Crete before, because she jealously guarded all the waters around her. But I was brazen enough to go as far as last night's island.'

'And tonight's island?'

'Is a much larger one, about the same distance as yesterday, called Kythira. Last night's island is called Antikythira, being south of the larger one.'

'And after Kythira?'

'Very little distance to the coast of the Peloponnesus.'

'What happens when we get there, merman?'

'We will probably be arrested first; Sparta protects its shores with spearmen rather than watchtowers. Then I shall ask for an audience with King Menelaus, your uncle. He owes you a duty of care until you are old enough to marry.'

Chryso's blue eyes are now focused entirely on mine; it never gets any easier to be near her blazing beauty. 'How old do women have to be before they can marry in Sparta, merman?'

'Twenty, my lady.'

'And I am but eighteen. Whom should I marry, merman?'

'You should make that choice, my lady, not I.'

'Then, will you marry me, merman?'

'With all my heart, my lady.'

*

My heart is full indeed as we approach our landfall. Surprisingly, the disciplined lines of bronze-armoured warriors on the beach look more like a welcoming committee than an arrest squad. A detachment of them comes forward to help us beach our ship. And with them is Paros, my foreman, whose shipbuilding operations I was called away from all that time ago to create the deadly horse of Troy. He greets me with a bear hug. 'Damian, you have been sorely missed! Welcome home, lad!' He registers my surprise with a grin. 'The Krypteia have had your ship in their sights since Antikythira. When I heard their description of you, I could hardly believe my ears. Had to see for myself!'

The Athenians are disembarking and being taken to horses for the men and small carriages for the women. Paros continues, 'We have had some intelligence about your crew, but you have a great deal to tell us! The king wishes you all to accept accommodation in the palace until suitable housing can be found for you, and,' he bows low at Chryso's approach, 'he and the queen are particularly eager to meet the princess, his niece!'

SEVEN

SEA POWER

Despite the unexpected warmth of the welcome that awaited us, I had been dreading arriving in Sparta because of the separation it would inevitably bring to Chryso and me. But it was not as bad as I had thought. King Menelaus and Queen Helen provided her with her own apartment in the palace, and she instantly became friends with their daughter, Hermione, who was a similar age. The girls had considerably more freedom than females in Athens and were allowed to ride out together and also visit the shipyard, where I was once more spending most of my time.

Paros, who was keen to put me up in his own home, soon informed me that warship building was more of a priority than ever in Sparta. The ships that had returned from Troy were in so poor a state that all had to be scrapped, and many had been lost on the journey home because of their lack of seaworthiness. This, sadly, did not surprise me in the least.

But it was Paros's second point that caught my attention, as we made our way to the shipyard a few days after my arrival. 'We have intelligence that Athens is not the only one to be increasing her naval strength; Mycenae is also hard at work building warships.'

That familiar coldness falls once more like a shadow across my mind as I ask, 'And who now rules Mycenae?'

'Princess Electra and her degenerate brother appear to be holding the reins now.'

'And what intelligence do we have on Crete? As we left, Knossos had a 150-foot wave heading for it, and that after a first wave which destroyed half her warships and all her trading vessels.'

Paros nods. 'I think that will have ruled her out of contention for dominance at sea for some time.'

'How large is our navy now?'

He smiles ruefully. 'Not as large as it would have been if we had not lost you, Damian. It stands at 150 biremes. The king would like to double that number.'

For some time now, ever since I built the horse in fact, ideas about a new kind of ship had been tapping insistently at a corner of my mind. Paros's words are like a door opening. I say, my face hot with shyness, 'I… I think I might be able to help.' And shortly afterwards, I am drawing in the sand again, with the same frantic energy that I had on Troy's shores and then on Crete's black beach. As I rush from stern to prow and back again, a small crowd starts to gather from the shipbuilding crews, among whom are now Pericles and his men, wanted far more by the navy than the army.

The words come tumbling out as I give shape to my ideas. 'The fundamental is that she will be faster and more manoeuvrable than our biremes. Instead of the two banks of oars, there will be three banks.'

Paros asks, 'And what will that do to the centre of gravity?'

I knew this would be the first question. 'It would remain low, master, because the ports would house the oarsmen with a minimal waste of space. There would be three files of oarsmen on each side, tightly but workably packed, by placing each man outboard of, and in height overlapping, the one below. The pins that act as fulcrums, allowing the oars to move, would be set inboard and overlap, keeping the centre of gravity low.'

'What would be her length?'

'One hundred and twenty feet, sir. So, fifty per cent longer than the bireme.'

'Number of oars?'

'One hundred and seventy.'

'So, considerably faster. By how much do you estimate?'

'On an average day, the oarsmen rowing for six to eight hours could travel more than sixty miles. On a good day, they could make one hundred miles.'

Paros frowns, and I can guess what is coming next. 'And what about a bad day, Damian? This ship, this trireme for want of a better name, is caught on top of a ten-foot wave, imposing a massive strain on her keel. What is going to prevent her from hogging?'

Hogging is the when the keel bends upwards, with the imminent risk of breaking. It is why, so far, the length of our warships has been limited to eighty foot. 'Two great cables, sir, each nearly two inches thick; rigged fore and aft from end to end along the centre line of the hull just under the main beams; tensioned by windlass to thirteen and a half tonnes force. These would be the real backbone of our trireme, as you are pleased to name it, sir.'

A buzz goes round the assembled workers. I add, 'The cable will act as a stretched tendon straight down the middle of the hull. As such, it will also significantly brace the hull structure against the stresses of ramming, giving us an important advantage in combat, sir.'

The workforce like this even more. There are quiet murmurs of, 'Sparta! Sparta!' And now, we hear a light, polite clapping. Princesses Chryso and Hermione have ridden quietly to the back of the crowd and are applauding, delighted smiles on their faces.

Paros bows to them. 'My ladies, do you think the king would give his approval to this new warship?'

The two girls exchange smiles, as Hermione says, 'I think he would like it very much; preferably, by tomorrow!'

Unlike most Greek states, Spartans are known for their respect for women, who are expected to speak out and be heard. At Princess Hermione's words, the shipyard workers break into spontaneous applause. Paros grins at me after the grilling he's given my idea. 'I think you can take that as a yes!'

*

Of course, that was just the initial go-ahead. I now had to provide detailed plans to show accommodations, propulsion, weight and waterline, centre of gravity and stability, strength and feasibility. I had to show how the trireme would be constructed to optimise all factors in its design, to the point where, if just one change was made, the entire design would be compromised. So, speed was maximised to the point where any less weight would have reduced the ship's structural integrity. The centre of gravity was placed at the lowest possible position where the lowest bank of oars was just above the waterline, which retained the ship's resistance to waves and rollover. If the centre of gravity were to be placed any higher, the additional beams needed to restore stability would have compromised hull space.

My two great cables were the subject of much debate between Paros and me. And I regret that I cannot impart to you the formula for their construction, because it was a secret as jealously guarded as was that of the Trojan horse. Suffice it to say that we formed two different teams and challenged them to compete to create the toughest cable ever designed. What is fascinating is that they each, in total secret, came up with exactly the same design, validating each other's idea, even before it was put to the test.

As the development of the prototype continues, Chryso and Hermione often come to observe our progress; the two girls have become like sisters. They even look like sisters, which is unsurprising as they are, after all, cousins. Hermione's hair is russet, and she has hazel eyes, but many of their facial expressions are similar, especially when they are approving of something. Which, thankfully with my new warship, they frequently are.

Paros and I are now joint managers of the project and spend a great deal of time together. He says, one day, as we watch the completion of the outer shell of the new vessel, 'I never wanted them to take you, Damian, but that choice wasn't mine.'

I look at him in surprise. 'Did you know why they wanted me, sir?'

'The Krypteia had brought word of your father's death. And they had news of the plan for the horse.'

'I am glad that you did not tell me.'

'It was a terrible task they gave you. And I am sorry for the loss of your father.'

'At the time, I felt very privileged to be entrusted with the horse, until I saw what Pyrrhos did to Priam and Astyanax and what he demanded for Polyxena.'

Paros shakes his head, as though he is trying to rid himself of visions of the slaughter. 'Spartans do not wage war in that way. I do not think that King Menelaus would have wanted Polyxena's death any more than he wished for the sacrifice of Iphigenia.'

I remember Epeios's giant head turning to me as he talked of bloodlust, and dimly, at the back of my mind, comes the shrieking laughter that I will never be entirely free of.

*

There is one essential aspect of my trireme's design with which, I have to confess, I am fairly obsessed. Too often, I have seen naval initiatives fail because of the lack of provisioning. Either they rely on supply lines that do not work, as at Troy, or foraging in the enemy country, which is a waste of manpower and also does not work, as at Troy, or they are trailed by a number of supply ships which slow them down and pose an obvious piracy risk. So, I design my trireme to utilise the abundant space beneath the fore and aft bulkheads to create room for provisions. With the low centre of gravity, the provisions will also act as ballast. And I go further. I talk to Chryso about honey bread; it is compact, keeps well and is packed with honey-powered energy. And while it is obviously not desirable for our crews to live solely off honey bread for too long, it could provide the solution to the provisioning. There will also be room for water supplies, although these are bulkier, but fresh water is more easily found than food when we have to island-hop. Chryso talks to Hermione, and she talks to her father, and soon, Sparta's bakeries are producing a whole new line in honey bread, called "Bread for Heroes". It sells out in hours, and they have to redouble production.

*

As soon as the prototype is completed, we begin to train oarsmen to row in three banks per side. This is the hardest task of all and critical to the trireme's speed and deathly delivery. I delegate this to Pericles and his men, remembering how well they dealt with it aboard *Pegasus*. In Crete, I was impressed by the Athenians' work ethic; in Sparta, they amaze me. Paros and I arrive at the shore to witness the first sea trial; a pan pipe plays as the oars dip and rise in perfect synchrony, and the hull races across the bay. I had always been optimistic about the speed of the trireme, but I had no idea that it could travel as fast as this. At the helm, Pericles gives me a cheerful wave.

A week later, with the ten-foot, bronze-clad ram attached to her prow at the waterline, the ship appears faster still; Paros concludes that the ram must effectively increase the trireme's length in the water and hence her speed.

Now I turn my attention to the sails. The bireme had just the one square mainsail. With the massive additional length of our trireme, we need to add a forward sail to help us steer and provide additional propulsion. So, I design a smaller mast that will be mounted on a forward slant just aft of the prow and lashed to the side stays; she will carry a highly manoeuvrable triangular sail which will help us turn through the wind as well as providing air power. I show the design to Paros and get the nod.

Next come the sea trials with the sails and the oars. The trireme is rowed across the bay against the wind; she is turned into the wind while the sails are hoisted; finally, with a shout of, 'Away!', she is turned so that the wind fills the sails. With a loud *crack!* the mainsail tightens, and the foresail goes taut. The oarsmen bend to it, and the ship accelerates at an extraordinary rate until she is tearing across the water. Cheers and applause come from the shipbuilders gathered to watch.

The following day comes the ultimate test, when our new warrior ship will show her capability as a destroyer. I am nervous about this, as the weather has turned completely foul. The skies have been darker ever since the fire mountain exploded, but the trials have to go ahead. And if the prototype is as seaworthy as I have designed her to be, she will be showing off more than just her power to ram and wreck. So, on a gloomy morning, with thunderclouds looming, we launch her; you do not use sails in combat – just 170 fully trained and super-fit oarsmen giving it their all.

I have set up three battered old boats for the prototype to destroy. They will be harder to wreck than seaworthy boats because they are already saturated with water and will tend to absorb the punishment. As lightning flickers across the bay and the first thunderclap roars, our ship gathers speed and charges on its prey, hitting it so hard amidships that it rolls over onto its side, a giant hole in its timbers. Showing off its tight turning circle, the trireme wheels round and accelerates towards victim number two; this time, it skewers the vessel in the stern. Again, the speed at which it hits is so great that maximum damage is done; the doomed ship is sinking stern first as its attacker wheels again and puts on top speed for its third charge. A sudden flash of sheet lightning illuminates the 120-foot-long destroyer as it hurtles towards the old cargo ship. There is a loud crash as the ram pierces the hull on the port side; the oarsmen keep rowing, and the old ship is pushed completely under the water, the warship with its shallow draft riding neatly over the top of the sinking vessel. With every hit, the crowd on the dockside gives a cheer, and as the warship sinks the third target, the chant rises like a drumbeat towards the black clouds: 'Sparta! Sparta!'

Paros says with a grin, 'Conclusive evidence of the strength of your cables, lad!' My main feeling is relief, as I had no idea that Pericles would try such a manoeuvre.

Then a hand drops onto my shoulder; turning, I see

the king himself and bow deeply. As Spartan kings are accustomed to leading their men to war, they wear the crimson military tunic and cloak far more often than regal clothing. So here is my king, dressed as a warrior and on foot. Behind him, Chryso and Hermione are riding fine Thessalian mares.

His tone is warm. 'I congratulate you, young master shipbuilder! Now, how quickly can you build one hundred of these mighty ships?'

Hermione laughs. 'I told you!'

*

With our new mandate, Paros and I gave the Athenians the roles of trainers for the elite teams who would build Sparta's new secret weapon. Then we set about establishing a volume production facility, whereby five ships could be built in parallel. Raw materials were the first priority, and the normal provisioning team was tripled in size and sent off to the forests with a long train of mule-drawn carts. Additional tanks for softening the wood were built and more builders and carpenters recruited to build the sloping sheds necessary to protect the new war fleet from the weather. In effect, Sparta's shipyards were about to expand to a size that would rival Athens' at Piraeus. And whereas Sparta's greatest strength had always been its army, now its navy too was to become a force to be reckoned with.

*

It took twelve intense, back-breaking months, with hundreds of shipbuilders working by daylight and torchlight in shifts to build one hundred triremes. In spite of the horrendous deadline, not one iota of quality was compromised; our team of inspectors let nothing slip by that was not one hundred per cent as it should be. Sea trials for every ship were rigorous, and King Menelaus insisted on attending with the princesses when each new warship was launched. I began to see how different he was in character from his brother Agamemnon.

In the month that we build the one hundredth trireme, King Menelaus invites Paros and me to dine with him and his family at the palace. Sitting at the table is his wife, Helen, who welcomes me warmly. Even after all she has been through, she is still a woman of great beauty. Not as beautiful as Chryso, but no woman in the world is. And nine years in Egypt under the protection of the Pharaoh, knowing that a completely futile war was being fought in her name, must have been beyond cruel. I begin to feel as sorry for Helen as I do for Orestes and Pyrrhos. All are Troy's victims; all have suffered.

Paros and I begin to get some hint of Menelaus's purpose after the women have gone to their sitting room. He says, 'Tell me about Princess Chrysothemis, Damian. There is a long history here and I feel I do not know all of it.'

'Gladly, sir. I will start with what you do know: it began with the sacrifice of her sister.'

Menelaus murmurs, 'I never wanted a child to be sacrificed so that the Greeks could sail to Troy. But my brother and his army were blood-hungry, and it could not be stopped.'

'No, sir. But all her life, Princess Chrysothemis will grieve for her sister.'

King Menelaus looks at me with eyes as bright blue as Chryso's. 'She tells me that she fled to Crete and put herself under the protection of King Idomeneo's household. And yet she was made to wait at table like a slave?'

'That was far from being the worst, sir. She had fled to Crete to escape the dreadful cycle of revenge that would lead, first, to her father's murder by his wife and her lover, and then to their murders by Electra and Orestes. Yet, King Idomeneo betrayed her whereabouts, and she was abducted from Crete. Electra took her back to Mycenae and would have killed her too, the same night that she and her brother murdered their mother.'

'If you had not saved her.'

'I should never have let them take her.'

'Against odds of two hundred to one, even a Spartan would have been a fool to attempt to fight.' King Menelaus turns to Paros. 'I have asked you both here tonight, not just to celebrate your achievements with our new warship fleet. We have had word from the Krypteia that Electra and her brother are planning to launch an attack on Crete, now that she is so weakened. We have been asked by King Idomeneo to render assistance.'

Paros says carefully, 'Am I correct in saying that you see an opportunity here, sir?'

'You are, Paros. I do not personally care if Idomeneo's kingdom disappears into the Aegean forever. But I do care about bringing murderers to justice.'

Paros looks at me. 'Is it likely that Princess Electra will personally lead the ships of Mycenae to war, Damian?'

'She was on the lead warship that came for Princess Chrysothemis, sir. The princess also once told me that her sister enjoys the act of killing, as a form of entertainment.'

The king's voice is calm. 'Her brother must stand trial too, if he can be found.'

I say to him, 'So you will be looking to bring them both to justice, sir?'

'Yes, Damian. In a Spartan court, justice will be done.'

*

We receive more intelligence from the Krypteia in the following days: Mycenae's fleet is more than three hundred warships strong and will be accompanied by one hundred provisioning ships. Paros and I look at a chart showing the extent of the voyage that Mycenae's ships will have to make. And I have an idea. 'We can form an advanced strike force. Swoop on their provisioning ships at night and cripple their supply lines.'

Paros nods. 'The king will like this approach. Now, we are called to a meeting with him. He has received intelligence on Crete.' On the way to the palace, Paros explains: 'The king wanted to be certain that Knossos is as weakened as Idomeneo says it is.'

'He feared that a trap was being set?'

'Indeed. He wants to talk to you about what you saw of Knossos's navy while you were in Crete.'

*

At the palace, we are shown into the throne room, where a young Krypteian officer waits to be questioned. King Menelaus himself is seated on a typically Spartan carved wooden throne with minimal adornment. He nods us over to two chairs at his side.

The king leads. 'You and your cohort have been carrying out surveillance of the port of Knossos?'

The young man bows. 'Yes, sir.'

'Did your investigations take you any further afield?'

'Yes, sir. We felt it would be useful to survey the fire mountain where the cataclysmic event took place that darkened the skies for many months afterwards.'

'Does this fire mountain have a name?'

'It is known to Cretans as Mount Thera, sir.'

'And what did you find when you investigated Mount Thera?'

The young man hesitates before replying. 'There was no mountain, sir. Just a sea, partially enclosed by a number of islands, in a circular pattern.'

King Menelaus looks at me. 'I heard from Princess Chrysothemis that you visited the fire mountain on your return from Mycenae?'

'That is correct, sir. This was a few weeks before the enormous eruption and the second great wave.'

'So, it would seem that Mount Thera literally blew itself to pieces?'

'It certainly looked and sounded like it, sir. I have never before seen such a sight or heard such a sound.'

'And the main recipient of the great waves would have been Knossos?'

'The northern shore would have been by far the most vulnerable, sir. We were extremely lucky in being sheltered by a promontory just to the east of the western coast.'

'Tell me what damage to the port you saw after the first great wave.'

'All the ships that had been afloat in the harbour had been wrecked, sir – warships and trading ships. Even the hundred or more warships being stored within sheds would not have escaped some damage.'

King Menelaus now turns back to the young Krypteian officer. 'Tell me what you saw in the port of Knossos.'

'So, this would have been maybe fourteen months after the second great wave, sir. We were hardly looking at a port at all. We could not see a single ship afloat. There were ships being constructed on the harbour sides, but these were in the very early stages.'

'Were there many men working in the port?'

'Very few, sir. It is possible that there was great loss of life when the second wave struck.'

'And the palace?'

'Being a substantial height above sea level, the outer walls of the palace looked intact, sir. But when we investigated the entrance to the labyrinth beneath, there was seawater lapping at the entrance. It looked as though the entire tunnel network was under water.'

His calm words make my blood run cold. How terrible would have been the results if we had not managed to evacuate the labyrinth and get well away from the northern shore. King Menelaus turns to Paros and me. 'Have you gentlemen any questions for the young officer?'

Paros says, 'Not for the officer, sir, but for Damian here. Did you say that you suspected that King Idomeneo could have been in league with Princess Electra and that is why he betrayed the whereabouts of Princess Chrysothemis to her and her brother?'

'At the time, I did suspect that, sir. But it is also quite likely that, with their former ally in a much-weakened position, they are now turning on him.'

The king looks at the young officer. 'Do you have any intelligence that could confirm or contradict these suspicions?'

'More than a year ago, we intercepted a messenger being sent from Knossos to Mycenae, sir. The message was coded but easy to decipher. It was a clear invitation to Princess Electra to abduct "she whom you seek" from his kingdom. But I'm afraid that at the time, sir, we did not know that Princess Chrysothemis was in Crete. So, we sent the messenger on his way.'

'You did what was in your power at the time. You have been most helpful. Please convey my thanks to your commander.'

The young officer bows and takes his leave.

The king is silent for a while as we all digest this news. Then he says to us, 'The Krypteia will be closely observing all that happens at Mycenae. They have a cohort permanently stationed there, which communicates regularly with our homeland security force. And so, gentlemen, what are your thoughts on this invading fleet?'

Paros nods at me and I say, 'I think we need to attack Mycenae rather than defend Crete, sir. Starting with an advance strike force, we can harry them as soon as they enter the Cyclades. The islands will give plenty of cover for us to attack, firstly, their provisioning ships.'

'Go on.'

'This will immediately make them weaker and unable to deploy their maritime forces effectively. If we sink all their supply ships, they will be forced to start island-hopping to reprovision.'

King Menelaus looks at me closely. 'There is a second part to your plan, isn't there, young master shipbuilder?'

'Yes, sir. They will not dare to land all their warships to reprovision because they will have to protect their backs from us. Even though their warships outnumber ours, we have the sea power to take on their rearguard ships. It may take a couple of attempts, but I think eventually, we will be able to trap their fleet and capture the princess and as many enemy ships as we can. We enslave their crews and enlarge our own fleet at Mycenae's expense. And we bring Princess Electra to justice.' This is by far the longest speech I have ever made, and I am breathless and hot with embarrassment by the end of it.

The king says gravely, 'I am deeply grateful that you escaped from Crete, young master shipbuilder. Because I see in you the makings of an admiral. What do you say, master Paros?'

'He will be a fine leader, sir.'

But I find myself horrified at the thought. 'Sir, with the greatest respect, I have worked under Paros's command all my life. I would much rather serve as his lieutenant!'

The king now smiles at the pair of us. 'And that you shall do! Admiral Paros and Vice-Admiral Damian, it is time to get to work!'

*

Our preparations for armouring our warriors and provisioning our ships are well underway, when we have an unexpected visitor. A single black sail appears on the horizon. At first, I experience a feeling of shock, wondering if this could be another abduction attempt by Electra, impossible though this would be in Sparta. But she and Orestes are not the only ones to fly sails of mourning. It takes maybe twenty minutes for the bireme to beach on our shores and be surrounded instantly by a military reception. A cohort of Spartan soldiers escorts Pyrrhos and his bodyguard towards the palace. Paros's grey eyes take in the copper-haired warrior as he strides, hand on the hilt of his sword, to a meeting with the brother of his former commander. 'At a guess, I would say that he wants to be part of our counter-offensive against Mycenae. The question is, should he be?'

The last time I saw Pyrrhos, he was calling for Polyxena's blood in that conference where, yet again, the winds howled for the sacrifice of a child. The time before that, we were sitting in the horse, and he was clenching his fists. Gathering the anger that would lead him to cut down the aged Priam as he sought shelter at the altar of Zeus; then, to throw the baby Astyanax out of a turret window to his death; and finally, to call relentlessly for the sacrifice of Priam's daughter so that she could join his father in the grave as his battle prize. An hour or so after today's encounter, Paros and I are summoned to the palace.

In the throne room, seated to the side of King Menelaus, Pyrrhos has changed. The shock of copper-coloured hair is slightly more bleached by the sun, doubtless from many battles. But the bold eyes that sought mine as he approached me that day on the beach, when others fled his company and I offered him food, are now haunted and bloodshot. He acknowledges me with a glance and a nod, as the king motions us to chairs.

King Menelaus leads. 'I am sure you agree that Prince Pyrrhos needs no introduction, gentlemen. His deeds of valour in the Trojan War are well known, as are those of his late father. The prince has come to us today to offer the services of himself and his Myrmidons, in our attempts to curb Mycenae's aggression against King Idomeneo of Crete. We are most grateful for this offer and recognise that in Prince Pyrrhos we would have a mighty ally. I would like to hear your views, as Admiral and Vice-Admiral of the Spartan fleet, as to how Prince Pyrrhos's forces could best be deployed.'

It is a simple question, so simple, that it would be easy to give an entirely wrong answer. Then, Paros's comment echoes in the back of my mind: 'Spartans do not wage war in that way.' Pyrrhos has but one agenda: vengeance. Even though his father, Achilles, bitterly hated Agamemnon, I can sense Pyrrhos's bloodlust; Electra and Orestes may have killed Agamemnon's murderers, but they too now deserve to die. Pyrrhos wishes to be that avenging angel. And once he gets anywhere near Electra, no one on earth will be able to stop him. He will make it impossible for us to bring her to justice, because he will enforce his own vision of justice by cutting her throat. King Menelaus knows this too.

In a flash, I can see how to thwart Pyrrhos in the most effective possible way. 'Sir, it is greatly to his credit that Prince Pyrrhos brings the valour of the Myrmidons to our aid. I would venture to suggest that the prince and his men would be most effectively deployed in blockading Knossos harbour; in this way, they can make absolutely certain that no Mycenaean warships can imperil King Idomeneo. I cannot think of any force that could better defend the king of Crete at his time of great need.' Slightly startled myself by my newly developed powers of flattery, I see a look in the eyes of King Menelaus that is at the same time relief and respect. Paros has the slightest hint of a grin. Pyrrhos's face is a mask; this is obviously not what he was hoping for, but there is nothing he can do about it.

King Menelaus brings the matter swiftly to a close with a gracious invitation. 'Prince Pyrrhos, I have a considerable debt of gratitude to you. In recognition of that, let us all dine together tonight. In the meantime, my housekeepers will see to it that you have suitable accommodation in the palace, to refresh yourself after your long journey.'

Paros's grin widens as we return to the dockyard. 'We see you have quite the makings of a statesman and a diplomat, Vice-Admiral Damian!'

'I just remembered something you said, sir, that's all.'

*

So, the Myrmidons beach their fifty ships on Sparta's shores, and their 2,500-strong military soon begin to impose a considerable strain on the hospitality of our citizens. But King Menelaus brings additional provisioners into the town to deal with the influx, and I am still more impressed by this king who is so clear in his purpose.

Paros and I are in our best Spartan crimson that evening. To my delight, I am seated opposite Chryso, who is looking even more dazzling than usual in a gold silk robe, down which her long hair shimmers. She and Hermione are seated next to each other, while Queen Helen is to the king's right and Pyrrhos to his left.

Hermione frequently steals glances at Pyrrhos; small wonder, because he is as handsome as his famous father was reputed to be, and he has made an effort for tonight, his broad shoulders robed in a cloak of purple silk clasped with gold at the neck. He is also making an effort with conversation to his neighbours, and from time to time, something approaching a smile lightens his fierce countenance. Frequently, too, I see him look at Hermione. I wonder if his visit to Sparta could result in more than one kind of alliance, and it chills me to think of Agamemnon's murderous deception, when he promised his daughter that she was to be married to Achilles, only to have her slain at the sacrificial altar. Can these old ties to the Furies ever be broken? Will those voices in my head ever cease?

Seated on my right, Paros mutters, 'They have put up the bodyguard in the barracks; apparently there are already some tensions.'

'Just as well that our forces will be fighting a long way from his when we join battle!'

At that point, my gaze is intercepted by a flash of blue from Chryso's eyes; glancing across at her, I read a clear approval for my Spartan crimson. My face must have gone the same colour as my cloak and tunic, because she giggles and whispers to Hermione. I am just happy that it's me she is looking at and not Pyrrhos; as for him, if he chances anything with Hermione's next-door neighbour, there could be some unseemly tensions at the banqueting table. But Pyrrhos has eyes only for the daughter of King Menelaus.

EIGHT
OUT OF THE DARK

In preparation for the Mycenaean invasion of Crete, Paros and I formed a special boat crew to reconnoitre our likely points of attack on the enemy fleet from the Cyclades islands. This crew was, of course, commanded by Pericles and consisted of his elite Athenians and hand-picked Spartan mariners. We had refurbished *Pegasus* after her voyage from Crete, and she made the ideal craft for a spy ship. I decided that her structure was robust enough to support a six-foot, bronze-clad ram, in case she needed to defend herself; by extending her length in the water, this also increased her speed. We furnished her with a larger sail, to take full advantage of the Etesian winds, and her crew conducted various sea trials to test her new abilities. She emerged as a swift, agile little ship, easy to beach and conceal on the Cyclades islands and with enough stowage for ample provisions.

Chryso and Hermione came to watch us launch the new *Pegasus*, Chryso explaining to Hermione what a huge part this little ship had played in our escape from Crete. And this gives me the chance to take Chryso to one side after the launch, to see if she can shed any light on a delay that is troubling me. The agreement we had arrived at with Pyrrhos was that he and his Myrmidons would sail before our fleet, head to Crete and mount the blockade of Knossos harbour. So, regardless of our success in containing the Mycenaean onslaught, whenever that happened, King Idomeneo would be protected. But the days passed, and still the Myrmidons did not sail.

Chryso glances across at Hermione as she chats with Pericles and his crew. 'Pyrrhos is now asking for Hermione's hand in marriage as a condition of allying himself with my uncle. He reminds Uncle of his "debt of gratitude". My uncle replies that we will see, once this battle is won.'

'What does Hermione want?'

'She is attracted to Pyrrhos but regards him as dangerous. She too wants to wait.'

'She is highly intelligent.'

'Oh, yes. Hermione is no one's fool!'

'And her father listens to her, doesn't he?'

'He listens to both of us. He has already agreed that I shall marry you, merman.'

I am almost lost for words. 'I thought… that he would want you to marry a prince.'

'He says the same as you: that I must decide who I marry.'

At this point, I realise that, despite my high regard for him, I have still been underestimating King Menelaus; he is so unlike his murdered brother as to not merit comparison with Agamemnon at all. It is also greatly to his credit that he so strongly desires to see justice done, that he is ready to commit Sparta's naval resources to bringing Electra and Orestes to book.

*

I want to make one more minor modification to *Pegasus*, involving the rudder arrangement. When this has been done, we wait until quite a strong wind is blowing, then row out to sea with a full complement of crew. My aim is to find out if the tweak to the rudder will improve our spy ship's performance in rough conditions. We sail in an easterly direction, towards the Cyclades, and I am feeling pleased – the modification has improved her ability to take the waves head on. I turn to Pericles to comment, but he is pointing ahead. 'Some trouble going on!'

Two ships are around half a mile away, one seeming to engage with the other. I know straight away what is happening. 'It's a pirate attack! To your oars!'

The two boats are being tossed around by the waves as we approach, but it soon becomes clear that the pirate ship is attempting to use grappling irons to pull the victim close so that they can board. I don't have any idea what we will do when we reach them, as our crew is completely unarmed. Or so I thought. Then Pericles dives under the bulkhead where we normally store provisions and comes out brandishing his hunting bow and arrow. Quick as a flash, he fires an arrow at the cutthroat handling the grappling irons. With a cry, the man drops the chain and clutches his arm. Pericles' second arrow hits the man behind, this time in the abdomen; he doubles up and falls on the deck.

I look at Pericles. 'Fancy trying out our new ram?' We are now about one hundred yards from the two ships; rowing like supermen, our marines quickly put on speed and in seconds we're tearing towards our target. They see us coming, but it's too late to do anything about it; we hit them broadside on, opening up a large hole just below the waterline of their hull. Now, the danger is that the dying ship will be thrust into the living one by the waves. I call to their helm, 'Throw us a line and we will pull you clear!' He is only too pleased to do so. Attaching the line to our stern, we row hard into the wind, and I can't help noticing how well the new rudder arrangement responds, even with a larger ship under tow behind us.

Once she is clear, I call again to the helmsman: 'Are you bound for Sparta? If so, we will take you there!'

A different voice calls back: 'We are bound for Sparta. I would be most grateful if you would convey us there!'

I have heard that voice before, when it was commanding Chryso to board his ship and come with him to certain death. It is Orestes.

Long before a foreign ship makes port in Sparta, our efficient lookouts ensure that there are always soldiers waiting to meet it. But there is no need for an armed presence with this Mycenaean ship. It is flying a white flag of surrender; everyone on board raises their hands to show that they carry no weapons; and Orestes, as soon as his feet touch the sand, kneels to me. 'I have heard that King Menelaus is seeking to bring me and my sister Electra to justice. I have come to give myself up.'

I say quickly to the Spartan commander, 'This is King Agamemnon's son, Orestes. If Prince Pyrrhos discovers that this man is here, he will not stop until he has slit his throat. He needs to go into protective custody under strict secrecy.'

The commander salutes, and Orestes is marched away, concealed under a hooded cloak. Pericles says thoughtfully, 'It was brave of him to do that.'

When I inform King Menelaus of our prisoner, he is silent for some time. Then, he says, 'It must be as if he is not here, until Pyrrhos and his Myrmidons are on their way to Crete. Otherwise, this terrible cycle of revenge will continue unchecked.'

'Is there a place where he can be kept in greater security than the prison, sir?'

'You say he has voluntarily surrendered himself? There is no risk of him fleeing?'

'All his actions in coming to Sparta unarmed and unprotected say that, sir, and so does he.'

'There is a safe house, at one of the local farms. Those who run the farm are retired security guards and completely trustworthy. I shall instruct my bodyguard to take Prince Orestes there and to replace him in the prison with a double, who shall also be clad in a hooded cloak.'

'That is a wise move, sir. He is in grave danger until Pyrrhos has left Sparta.'

King Menelaus says reflectively, 'Which, so far, he has shown little sign of doing.'

In fact, Pyrrhos has shown absolutely no sign that he intends to carry out his side of the agreement with King Menelaus. With the presence of 2,500 Myrmidons in Sparta, and our beaches choked with their ships, despite the legendary restraint of Spartan soldiers, tensions are perceptibly rising. So, it is a huge relief when, on the following day, a young Krypteian officer stands in front of King Menelaus, Pyrrhos, Paros and me in the throne room with the long-awaited news. 'The Mycenaean fleet sailed southwards three days ago, sir.'

'Their numbers as previously reported?'

'Yes, sir. Three hundred warships, one hundred provisioning ships.'

King Menelaus looks at me and Paros. 'Then the wolves had better get after them!'

We bow and leave. Our spy ship *Pegasus*, with Pericles at the helm, sails immediately, and our warships within two hours. I heard afterwards that Pyrrhos sailed southwards the next day; our departure in effect forced his. His position would have been ignominious indeed if he had delayed any longer. Sparta was running out of patience with the thuggish Myrmidons, and Chryso hinted to me that Hermione was entirely out of patience at being treated as a bargaining chip by her would-be husband.

I also privately reflected that Menelaus cared not one iota if Pyrrhos went to protect Knossos port or not; he must simply have been delighted that he was gone, without having discovered that Orestes was awaiting Spartan justice, not the vengeance of the old gods of hate and rage.

*

Our fleet consists of all one hundred triremes and the existing 150 biremes, manned by highly trained, fighting-fit marines straining at the leash to chase the prey. A special contingent of ten triremes has been designated to mount the pre-emptive night strikes on the Mycenaean supply ships. The entire fleet will be deployed when we succeed in driving the Mycenaeans to reprovision.

With the ten-ship contingent at the head of the fleet, Pericles, commander of the spy ship, will alert us in daylight by flying a red military cloak on his mast as soon as he spies a target. By night, he will fire a torch. At this point, the ten-ship contingent will leave the fleet, which will beach on the nearest island and await further orders.

We sail on a broad reach, wind power taking us on an easterly course towards the Cyclades, through which the Mycenaean fleet must pass. Evening is drawing in as we follow Pericles' spy ship into the lee of a small island. His torch flashes once, twice. He has sighted the beginnings of the enemy fleet. They will be led by their warships, which will be looking to make landfall before a dawn resumption of their course. The trireme contingent slips away to join up with Pericles, as he waits, almost invisible in the gathering dark. We let the warships through. The last one has almost disappeared, the slower provisioning ships following at the back of the line.

Then we strike. In a series of shock and awe attacks, our ten triremes pick them off five at a time. Tearing out of the night, each warship rams a supply ship broadside on at full speed with a lethal blow to its hull; then it wheels and repositions itself for the next charge, while the trireme behind it deals destruction to the following supply ship. In just over an hour, we take out twenty-five of these ships and there is nothing they can do to defend themselves. The warships ahead can have no idea that wolves are savaging the rear of their fleet.

As we regroup, I look at Paros. 'Shall we go again, sir?'

'We go again, Vice-Admiral. And again.'

The sun is long since set, and for our first assaults the night sky was overcast. But now a full moon sheds a silvery light on the waters and illuminates the seventy-five supply ships remaining. In the previous darkness they may have seen little of the commotion; now, even in the moonlight, the sheer speed of our charges makes them utterly helpless. Again and again, our mighty triremes turn the heavily loaded supply ships into splintered, sinking wrecks. Dawn is trailing faint dusky-pink clouds across the eastern skies, when the sea to the farthest horizon has been emptied of any ship that is not Spartan.

We give the signal to the strike force to return to the main fleet; we will now sail southwards on the path of the Mycenaean warships. Pericles and his crew will tail the enemy fleet, to see where they make landfall. On meeting up with their fleet, our mariners first take some well-deserved food. With the coming of the sun, the Etesians are starting to blow and give some much-needed rest to our strike force. Sails fill and go taut; seabirds wheel and cry overhead; and the mighty fleet of Spartan triremes is on the move to hunt down Princess Electra of Mycenae and bring her face to face with justice.

That day soon turns into one of heavy squalls and gusting wind. By mid-afternoon, we are forced to reef the sails, which are at risk of being torn apart, so violent are the gusts. My consolation is that we must be making better headway than Mycenae's fleet because of our superior speed in the water. We press on as night falls, and gradually the storms die down. At first light the following day, we see a small ship on the horizon waving a red cloak as a flag. Pericles must have found the enemy fleet.

'They have diverted to Naxos. At first, they landed on Sifnos, presumably as a staging point before regrouping for the final leg to Crete. But then they began to realise that they had lost their supply ships. We had beached in a neighbouring cove and climbed the cliff to observe them. It was sheer mindless panic. Some thought that the ships had gone down in the storms. Others, that they had been attacked by pirates – a reasonable assumption. No one ever mooted the possibility of Spartan wolves on their tail. Anyway, one thing was evident: Sifnos did not have the capability to reprovision their fleet. The word went round that they would have to divert from their chosen course and go to Naxos. While they were readying their ships, we scrambled back down the cliff and slipped away to bring you the news.'

Paros's grey eyes look eastwards; Naxos is more or less a left turn from here. 'If they have no idea that it is Sparta who is wreaking this havoc, we may find our task easier than we thought.'

'Because most of their ships will be beached?'

'Far easier than reprovisioning in the water. But they had better have plenty of gold, silver and diplomacy! Naxos is the largest of the Cyclades islands and fiercely independent. A large Mycenaean fleet arriving on their shores will be judged an invasion.'

'So, we had better keep their whole operation under close surveillance before deciding what we must do.'

Paros nods. 'Our ships need to stand off well out of sight at Pelos, to the north. That way, we can make use of the Etesians to get to Naxos quickly when the time comes.'

Pericles says, 'With your permission then, sir, we will get back on their tail.'

NINE

OLD GODS

I go with Pericles to chase the Mycenaeans to Naxos, while Paros takes charge of our main fleet and follows on, bound for Pelos. Ours is a fast trip on a beam reach almost all of the way; by evening, the mountainous shores of Naxos are looming on the horizon. We steer clear of the main harbour, where the Mycenaean fleet will be aiming to dock; to what kind of reception, we intend to find out.

Rowing round the headland, we find a small cove, pull *Pegasus* well up onto the beach and hide her behind rocks. Then, leaving the rest of the crew to guard the ship and take some food, Pericles and I climb the cliff. From the top, we can look down on Naxos's expansive port, which is set into a bay around a mile across. Naxos's navy is in port, consisting of around a hundred biremes drawn up onto the sand, just below the sheds that would normally house them. A full complement of marines, armed to the teeth, stands with each ship. Pericles whispers, 'It looks like they are preparing for action.' It is not hard to guess what kind of action. The Mycenaean warships wait in serried rows at the mouth of the bay; they number now around 250 so must have suffered heavy losses in the storms. In the middle of the bay, two ships – one Mycenaean, one Naxian – lie alongside each other while their two admirals talk.

The talks continue for at least twenty minutes; then we see many bags of coin, presumably silver and gold, being handed over to the host. But the negotiations are not over yet. A personage in a regal purple cloak is taken hostage onto the Naxian ship and unceremoniously tied to the mast; Naxos knows that Mycenae is rich so can easily afford the payment; Naxos knows too that Mycenae is duplicitous.

The Mycenaean ships are now allowed to advance in groups of ten at a time, to load supplies that are brought to the harbour side. Throughout the proceedings, the Naxian marines remain on station. This will take most of the night; Pericles and I have seen enough. Hurrying back to our little ship, we set course for Pelos to meet up with the Spartan fleet. We find them preparing to beach in a peaceful bay on the island's leeward side. Sitting down with Paros, Pericles and I tell him what we have found.

He muses, 'This is an interesting conundrum, isn't it? While goods are being traded, Naxos is technically an ally of Mycenae. So, if we attempt to blockade their port, we will have two enemy fleets aligned against us.'

I can see no option. 'We have to let her resupply and sail. They will be slower with supplies aboard that their warships were never designed to take. And their numbers now are much reduced – they almost exactly match ours.'

Pericles says, 'So we aim to ambush them, like we did with the supply ships?'

Paros comments, 'They will not be such a soft touch.'

'No, master. But what if we mount a pincer action? We know what their course to Crete will be. Starting now, half of our fleet goes at top speed to, say, Mount Thera, and lies in wait; they will get there comfortably ahead of the heavily loaded and later-departing enemy ships. The rest of the fleet tails the Mycenaeans until Thera is in sight; then we all close in on them from behind and in front. If we surround them in that way, we are far more likely to get them to surrender rather than try to fight it out.'

Paros's grey eyes have a humorous glint. 'By Zeus, lad, I like it!'

And so, the Spartan trap was set. Paros and I quickly briefed all the commanders and he elected to lead Pincer Alpha, as we called the first half of the fleet, while I followed the Mycenaeans with the wolves who would soon be snapping once again at their heels.

*

I worked out that it must be around seventy miles from Pelos to what remained of Mount Thera. We had verified that our new triremes could, even on an average day, cover the same distance; if we assume that he will have an average night, Paros has no need to hurry. In the meantime, Pericles returns with our spy ship to Naxos and watches. I set a scout ship to row out a half mile or so to where it can clearly see his signal that the Mycenaeans have departed. At the first light of dawn, the scout ship fires a flaming arrow skywards. In tightly disciplined formation, my fleet of 124 warships now follows, the scout ship remaining ahead so that it is the only ship that might be sighted by the enemy.

Of course, there is no such thing as an average day or night in the Aegean. By midday, the sun has disappeared behind a massive bank of cloud, so low that it feels claustrophobic beneath it. The wind rises to a howl, propelling the fleet forwards so quickly that we hastily reef the sails to try and stabilise the ships. Even with the sails reefed, we are travelling at breakneck speed; the wind is so loud that it shuts out all other sound. The lowering cloud has now created a daytime night as we speed on into the dark. Then, stark against the thin strip of light horizon remaining, I see a phenomenon that I have never before encountered. A dark, twirling funnel extends from the cloud down to the sea. A severe test of our triremes' seaworthiness is about to commence, as we are swept helplessly towards the waterspout.

I can understand why mariners sometimes tell stories of giant sea snakes that engulf ships. This monster looks just like a vast, writhing serpent and its roaring is louder even than the wind. Forked lightning shoots from cloud to sea as the funnel whirls towards us. Then it is on us, and we are within its maw, the ship rocked with the force of the torrents of water filling the hull. It is like being battered by rocks from an avalanche. As quickly as it arrived, the beast passes through our fleet, but still we cannot stop to render help where it may be needed. Only when the winds finally drop, and we are suddenly becalmed, do I have time to assess the damage that has been done.

As we inspect the fleet, we see frantic bailing, and we rescue fifteen lost oars floating in the waters. Three ships have been dismasted. But not a single ship has been seriously damaged, and my crews look unhurt, if somewhat stunned, by what hit them. I wonder if Paros's fleet encountered the spout; with his vast experience he has probably met sea serpents before. I, for one, hope that this is our first and last time.

*

Once their oars are restored, the three dismasted ships are now seaworthy again; they won't need their sails to fight, and their crews are uninjured bar a few bruises. The scout ship is in position around a mile in front of us. I decide that the whole fleet should now proceed by rowing only, since we must be nearing Mount Thera, so rapid has been our progress under that fierce wind power. Sure enough, within one hour, Pericles flies a red cloak from his mast. He now halts and waits for us to join him. As we do so, we too see the Mycenaean fleet ahead and, beyond it, the dark peaks of the ruins of Mount Thera. There is no way of knowing if Paros is waiting with his fleet, ready to attack their front; we just have to trust that his warships have arrived safely and are ready to strike.

With my fleet now in tight formation, I give the order

to charge, and we row at full speed for the rear of the Mycenaean pack. We have some help from the following wind and our speed is as great as it has ever been. Within minutes, our first triremes are skewering the enemy in the stern with a single massive blow beneath the waterline, then wheeling away to make room for the following ships. Each trireme then moves up the sides of the Mycenaean fleet to charge again and hit them broadside on. This extremely fast shock and awe tactic works so well that it is some minutes before the Mycenaeans realise that they are under attack. Even then, there is little that they can do about it. You can't start a rearguard action while you are advancing, and their ships at the front have no idea at all what is coming at them from behind. To make things worse for Electra's fleet, their ships are made far less manoeuvrable by the weight of the provisions they took on board at Naxos. That same weight makes them sink rapidly, seconds after our triremes have punched a huge hole in their hulls.

Pericles' scout ship has been observing from the sidelines while this onslaught takes place. After half an hour, he comes alongside us and calls, 'Pincer Alpha is engaging them from the front, sir!' And my heart thuds with excitement that, so far at least, our plan is working. It is working quickly, too. Paros's ships are doing what ours are; as soon as a line has charged and rammed head-on, they wheel and attack Mycenae on its flanks. Hampered in taking evasive action by the weight of the supplies they have taken on, and now being attacked on all four sides at once, Mycenae's ships are in complete disarray. Their only way of defending themselves would be to form a square, with each of the four sides facing our ships. But even then, they are packed together so tightly that they would lack the room to manoeuvre, and they have been taken so much by surprise that no one seems to be thinking about what they do to fight back. I wonder if Electra has appointed herself admiral of this fleet or whether they have an admiral at all.

In very little time, with more than one hundred of their ships splintered and sunk, they are completely surrounded and unable to move. Then I see Paros's ship rowing down the enemy ranks; he is ordering them to surrender, first their queen, Electra, then themselves and their ships. We take the opposite flank and convey the same orders. White flags are run up the masts across what is left of the Mycenaean fleet. But of Electra, there is no sign. Pericles runs alongside us once more. 'They say that their queen is not with them.'

We sail with our prisoners to the port of Knossos, a journey that takes two days. Here, we are unsurprised to note the absence of Pyrrhos and his Myrmidons. We are warmly welcomed by King Idomeneo and feasted in the palace, our men being well looked after in more humble accommodation. And here, Paros puts forward an offer to the king which makes a lot of sense: 'Sir, here are one hundred or so captive enemy ships, fully crewed with men you can enslave and use to replace your own much-depleted manpower. We have sustained minimal damage and, so far by the grace of the gods, no losses. I know that King Menelaus would be of the same mind as we are.'

King Idomeneo smiles graciously. 'It is an offer, Admiral Paros, which I am delighted to accept. Please convey my gratitude to your king.'

Later, when King Idomeneo has absented himself, Paros and I have a chance to talk. 'What are your thoughts on the missing queen, Vice-Admiral?'

'Ships have been searched and crews interrogated. We have to believe them.'

Paros's grey eyes look at me closely. 'I can guess what you may be thinking. She is not necessarily still in Mycenae, is she?'

'No, sir. I am deeply worried that she may be in Sparta.'

'So, you fear for the safety of Princess Chrysothemis?'

'Yes, sir. And also for Orestes.'

*

We muster the crews early the next morning. King Idomeneo has fulfilled all our requests for the provisions that we need, and they are now being rapidly loaded. I brief our crews, as they stand by their ships. They can see that something is to be asked of them that is bigger than anything they have done before. I stand before them. 'You have made Sparta victorious, beaten Mycenae beneath the waves. But a deadly danger is now in our homeland. The murdering Queen Electra is at large there, and her foremost aim is to kill her sister, Princess Chrysothemis. We must get back to Sparta in the shortest possible time: I am asking you to row non-stop, against the Etesian winds, for 175 miles. Are you with me?'

Spartans have a reputation for being silent, deadly types. But there is nothing quiet about the roar that goes up from these men. Chryso and Hermione are beloved by them because of the firm support they have always given to Sparta's navy. The two princesses make almost daily appearances at the shipyards. Every man here will give all he has to this epic run.

Just before I board my ship, King Idomeneo takes my arm and steers me to one side. He says, 'I am truly grateful for what Sparta has done for Crete, Vice-Admiral Damian. And I bitterly regret aiding Electra and her brother in their murdering quest for Princess Chrysothemis. It must have been a kind of madness.'

I shake his hand. 'Yours are brave words, King, and I thank you for them. Your family gave shelter to Princess Chrysothemis for a long time. It is now up to Sparta to preserve her life by bringing her sister to justice.' Minutes later, our ships are rowing out of the port of Crete as though we have demons on our back. The real demon is 175 miles away, but I have never seen men row like this.

Taking an oar side by side with my crew, I develop blisters that have no time to heal. Muscles are screaming; bones feel as though they are about to break; throats are dry for hours; and guts are glued to our spines, before food and drink are grabbed without a pause in the rowing. But there is an excitement among the crew that fires everyone, making us immune to the pain of straining muscles and blistered hands; we are doing something that has never been done before. Night falls and we row on; the goddess Selene is kind, and gentle moonlight tops the waves ahead of us. As we pass the island of Antikythira, I call to them, 'No one has ever done Sparta from Crete non-stop!'

Dawn raises pale light in the east as we pass Kythira, and I shout to my crew, 'You will shortly beach on Sparta's shores; you are all heroes!' I think they can hardly believe that we have come such a long way in such a short time; I can hardly believe it myself. Briefly, I entertain the idea of running a giant race annually from Crete to Sparta, to see if anyone can beat our record. When we finally beach, it stands at twenty-two hours. Waiting to welcome us is an army of Spartan warriors, headed by the king himself and the two princesses, each on horseback.

Bowing deeply to the princesses and to King Menelaus, I say, 'I regret that Electra has evaded us, sir. She may be at large in Sparta.'

The king knows immediately what this could mean. Turning to the army commander, he says, 'The princesses must each have a bodyguard at all times. Redouble security at the safe house. And begin a search of every house, every farm, every barn.'

Then Chryso jumps down from her mare and comes forward, blue eyes blazing. 'Be aware of how clever my sister is! She may be disguised as a man. As a woman, she would be conspicuous, but as a man, looking for work, say, in the dockyard?'

The king says to the army commander, 'Go back through your records of all strangers who have come to our shores in recent months. Check with the wardens at the safe house to see if they have observed any potential intruders.'

I rack my brains to try and think of anything I might

have missed, but I can't think straight. Taking my leave of the king and the princesses, I stumble to Paros's house and sleep for a few hours. But the sleep is fraught with uneasy dreams. The following morning, I remember what I should have thought of and race to the jail. There is a guard around it with swords drawn and I know, from the face of the chief warder, that I am too late. The prisoner who was doubling as Orestes in the cloak and hood has been stabbed to death during the night.

The Furies howl once more in my head as I make my way on leaden feet to the palace. Electra is closing in; invisible, untouchable, unstoppable. Once just a remote presence on faraway shores, she swooped like a vulture to spirit away Chryso when it pleased her, and I was powerless to prevent her. Now, with that same effortless ease, she is coming at us again out of the dark; she seems so close, it makes me feel deathly cold.

King Menelaus is with his daughter and his niece. He has heard the news from the prison.

'I blame myself, sir. I should have known that would be the first place she would go.'

Hermione says, 'What could you have done, Damian? They cannot understand how she got in.'

Chryso replies, 'She is a master of disguise. Sometimes, she would pretend to be a page boy or a slave, just to check up on the servants. She liked to have eyes everywhere!'

King Menelaus is reassuring. 'All that can be done, is being done. The army are scouring town and countryside. Every citizen is being warned to be on their guard and report directly to the military if they see anything to arouse suspicion. Now, take some food with us, Vice-Admiral. You look extremely pale.' As he speaks, a grey-haired housekeeper brings in cold meats and bread on platters and sets them on the dining table. She disappears and comes back in a few minutes with a flagon of wine.

Chryso asks her, 'Can you bring water, too, please?'

The woman nods in a brief bow and turns to go. King Menelaus says reprovingly, 'Do you not know how to reply to a request from a princess? Answer her properly!'

The woman gestures towards her throat, as though trying to explain that she cannot speak. In that flash of a second, I know why she does not wish to utter a word. The voice is the hardest thing of all to properly disguise. Seeing me, she realised that the game would be up if she spoke. Jumping up so fast that I knock my chair over, I grasp the woman's wrist as she tries to flee and pin it behind her back in an iron grip that not even a Fury could escape. 'Do not touch anything she has served!'

She spits and kicks and writhes and fights me with grotesque strength until, within seconds, the guards arrive to take her away. All colour drained from her face, Chryso stares after her sister. She whispers, 'Even if she had spoken, I would not have recognised her.'

*

That afternoon, I ride to the safe house. It is an unassuming little farmhouse with fields of sheep contentedly nibbling. The guards who had been protecting Orestes night and day from his sister have now departed. The chief warden greets me and takes my horse. I say tentatively, 'I would like to sit outside with him, if you consider that appropriate.'

He smiles grimly. 'It could be the first time in quite a while that he has done that!'

'How has he been since he has come here?'

'He is very courteous to everyone. But he looks haunted. He eats and drinks little; I think he wishes to quit this world.'

'Would it be possible for someone to bring us some bread and wine while we sit outside?'

'It would do him good to take some.'

The last time I saw Orestes, he was kneeling on the sand before me, head bowed, surrendering himself to Spartan justice. The time before that, he was sitting at the banquet which was to precede the murder of his mother and her lover; he looked as though he wished the earth would swallow him up. Now, as he is led towards me through the small courtyard outside the farmhouse, I am shocked at how gaunt he is. I stand as he approaches and motion him to the seat beside me. We sit, and bread and wine are brought to the small table between us. The sun is gentle, and birdsong soars over the fields. I say nothing for a while, giving him time to get used to being outside in the sunlight, when he has been in darkness for so long.

Then, I pour us each some wine and take a sip of mine, aware, in my Spartan way, that this is something I must be very careful about. I pass him his goblet. He takes it but hesitates, as though he does not deserve the wine. 'Drink – you need it!'

Obediently, he takes a sip. Almost immediately, some colour returns to his face. I say to him, 'I am come to tell you that your sister Electra presents no more danger to you or to anyone else. She is in custody here in Sparta and will be brought to trial.'

His voice is as I remember it but steadier now. 'And I too will be brought to trial, I hope?'

'Yes. It will be a fair trial. Sparta's justice system goes back a long way, to our ancient lawgiver, Lycurgus.'

He takes another sip of the wine. I push the bread towards him, and he takes a piece and bites into it. After a long pause, he says, 'If I say that I murdered our mother and her lover, will you let Electra go free?'

'I cannot speak for the judges.'

'She will deny all guilt. She will say that I stabbed them. It could be easier for us all if I confess to it.'

'Did you kill them?'

'No. She ordered me to, but I could not.'

'You must tell the truth. You must not become another of her victims.'

'It will be my word against hers – who will believe me?'

'Did anyone see anything at all of what happened?'

His eyes close for a second, as he relives the terror. Then he stares ahead of him, remembering. 'Electra had to change her dress afterwards. It was covered in blood. A maid came and was told to take the dress and burn it. She must have seen the bodies.'

I get up. 'This maid must be found. She *will* be found!'

'Would anyone believe a servant girl?'

'Females are regarded differently in Sparta, brother.'

A half smile spreads across his features. 'Brother… none of my sisters ever called me that.'

'I will soon have the great privilege of marrying Princess Chrysothemis and of calling you brother every day if you can put up with it!'

'May I see her?'

'The king will come with her tomorrow. In the meantime, you must eat and drink and live!'

*

Pericles and I debate how best to approach the mission to Mycenae. We decide that speed has priority over stealth and take an abundantly provisioned trireme powered by 170 fully armed marines. We leave that evening and row through the night and all the following day, beating against the Etesians blowing from the north. The only pause is when we pull into a cove to wait out a hammer blow of a squall which suddenly barrels out of nowhere, allowing the men to eat and drink their fill and catch an hour's sleep.

On the third morning, we arrive in the gulf of Aulis. Leaving a contingent of seventy men to guard the ship, we do a forced march all that day; by evening, we are beneath the towering ramparts of the castle and the massive stone lions of the main entrance. I say impatiently to Pericles, 'This is no time for civilities; we are going in via the secret entrance.' We lead our squadron of one hundred Spartans up through the tunnel, into the servants' quarters and then down into the main hall. In the total anarchy that must have prevailed since the murders and the subsequent disappearance of Electra and Orestes, the staff have been making merry. The carousing at the banqueting tables comes to an abrupt halt when they find themselves surrounded by bronze-armoured soldiers, swords at the ready. I ask them, 'Where is your chief of staff?'

One middle-aged man who looks only slightly less drunk than the others stands up and sways, blubbering, 'Have mercy, sirs… we have done no wrong.'

'And no wrong will be done to you if you co-operate. We seek the maidservant who attended Princess Electra the night that the queen and her paramour were murdered.'

'Ah… then you will not find her in here. She thinks herself too grand to keep company with us since that night.'

Pericles mutters, 'More likely she is simply terrified!'

I order the blusterer, 'Send for her. Tell her she will be treated well.'

A serving girl hurries out. No one dares move while the marines stand there motionless, the firelight reflecting in their bronze armour, their faces hooded by their cockaded helmets. Some of the staff exchange uneasy looks, and I wonder what other crimes may have been committed on that night of double murder. The girl returns in a panic. 'I am sorry, sirs, I can find Melitta nowhere!'

I order the party goers, 'You will all remain exactly where you are!', while Pericles commands the marines to search the palace.

I say to him, 'I have an idea that I know where she is.' We run to the royal apartments on the floor above the servants' quarters. The door to the room where they had tied up Chryso is open. The door next to it, to the late queen's bed chamber, is closed. I knock and say softly, 'We come as your friends.' The door opens quietly on well-oiled hinges;

Electra must have prepared the ground well. She probably drugged the couple's wine to ensure that they would not wake.

When Pericles and I enter, we stand still in complete shock. I will try to spare you too much detail, but for the sake of the truth, however horrifying it may be, this has to be told. The bodies have been removed, but the room is still a scene of slaughter. Blood is everywhere, now dried to a pale brown; staining the pillows, the sheets, the tapestried carpets; smearing the walls. The bedsheets are in horrible disarray, showing signs of desperate struggle. I remember how unnaturally powerful the Fury was when she fought to escape me. Even the two of them against her would have stood no chance. And there, in the corner, petrified and weeping quietly, is our little witness, barely more than a child; she clutches in her arms the brocaded gold silk robe that Chryso and I saw Electra wearing the night we fled this castle of death; little of the gold can be seen beneath the veil of dried blood.

Pericles goes to her and kneels beside her, putting a gentle arm around her. 'Little one, are you Melitta?'

She turns a tear-stained face to him and nods, still shaking with sobs. He says softly, 'We have come to take you to a safe place where you will be looked after with kindness. But first you must give this terrible robe to my friend here and bear it with you no more.'

She lets me take it, as though a curse has been lifted from her. Pericles lifts her up in his arms like an infant, and we leave that awful room. Giving commands to the marines outside to summon their colleagues and swiftly follow us, we pass through that dark corridor, down the steps to the servants' quarters, from there to the tunnel and finally into the fresh night air. I am sure that, to a man, our marines were glad to quit that dreadful castle and place their feet back on the road towards the sea. Exhausted, and lulled by the rhythmic marching, the child falls asleep in Pericles' arms, and I think of those two other children, Iphigenia and Polyxena, who could not escape the merciless gods like she has.

During all that long voyage back to Sparta, Pericles is like a father to the little girl; he gives her honey bread and water, coaxing her to eat and drink; he tells her stories of the sea and finally makes her smile; and he provides a cosy little bed beneath the bulwarks where she can curl up and sleep. While she is sleeping, he takes an oar with me and tells me about Melitta. 'She has been in that room ever since the murders; only coming out at night to steal down into the kitchen for some scraps. She says Electra told her to burn the dress, but she was too afraid to, in case her mistress changed her mind. She was regularly beaten by Electra and treated like a pariah by the staff. She has been utterly friendless.'

When we dock in Sparta, King Menelaus is once again there to receive us; gently, he welcomes Melitta. Then, Pericles takes the little girl to his own home which is now to be her home too. He told me the news on the voyage back. 'Athena and I have become the proud parents of a baby boy. We will have a big sister for him!'

*

Trials in Sparta are usually run by the military and presided over by a panel of Elders. But King Menelaus feels that there is more on trial here than a murderer. Paros and I are sitting at supper in the palace with the king, his queen and the princesses. The king says thoughtfully, 'We can now prove conclusively that the murders were carried out by Electra. But, if she admits to her guilt, she is also likely to say that she was justified.'

'That she was avenging the murder of her father, your brother, sir?'

'Yes, Damian.'

'What do the laws of Sparta say about murder, sir?'

'If she was being tried in Athens, they would very likely consult the oracle at Delphi. Here, we work to military law; it is against the law to kill, unless you are defending your country in battle.'

'So, Electra must be judged by the laws of the country in which she is being tried.'

'She must do that, but the trial must give her a fair hearing.' The king looks at his wife and the princesses. 'I would value your views, my ladies.'

Chryso says, 'Could she have an advocate to speak for her?'

King Menelaus nods in approval. 'I will put this to the ephors, who will form the panel of Elders.'

Hermione says suddenly, 'If Electra is to have an advocate, then surely Orestes should have one too!'

'That would seem only fair.'

Hermione pursues her point. 'And surely, each should be able to choose their own advocate?'

The king replies gravely, 'You have given me a great deal to think about. I will consult the ephors at the earliest opportunity.' He turns to his wife. 'Your daughter and your niece have a fine appreciation of the cause of justice, my lady.'

Queen Helen smiles and a radiance shines from her eyes that gives me a glimpse of the beauty that sent all those ships to Troy. 'They do indeed, my lord. They make me very proud of them.' And suddenly, the injustice that kept her a prisoner in Egypt all those long years cuts me through; far away from her daughter and her husband, she must have suffered greatly. Yet another victim of Troy, amid a total absence of victors.

On the way back to his house, Paros remarks, 'Of course, it's really the gods who are on trial here, isn't it?'

'Don't you think it's about time?'

'They have a lot to answer for! The king was right about Athens; they would likely have let Electra off, saying it was Apollo's will that Agamemnon be avenged.'

'And there is Pyrrhos, his whole life driven by the quest for vengeance for his father. The only one left to him now is Apollo, who is said to have guided the arrow of Paris. What chance has Pyrrhos of getting justice from a murdering deity?'

*

The next day, Hermione asks if she can accompany her father to see Orestes and offer him an advocate. Chryso wants to see her brother again, and she wants me to be there too. So, the afternoon sun warms the four of us sitting in the garden with Orestes. He is now far from the thin, haunted youth whom I was urging to eat and drink two weeks ago; animated and alert, he has a light in his eyes that was not there before.

King Menelaus explains how Chryso came up with the idea of an advocate for Electra and how Hermione felt that he should have one too. 'My dear sister, that is very good of you.' He turns to Hermione. 'My lady, it was very kind of you to think of me.'

Hermione replies firmly, 'It was only just and fair!'

Chryso affectionately leans across and takes his hand. 'You were never very good at sticking up for yourself, little brother!'

Hermione says, 'Is there someone in particular you would like to speak for you, cousin?'

He murmurs, 'I… have no friends… except for my future brother-in-law…' Standing, he looks at me with that light in his eyes.

I stand and shake his hand firmly. 'I will be honoured to speak on your behalf, brother. And you will find that you have many friends!'

The next day, we find out who is Electra's choice of advocate. She wants King Odysseus of Ithaca to speak on her behalf. If he agrees, I am to confront the wiliest and most eloquent orator in the world across the courtroom.

TEN

ODYSSEUS

Pericles and I leave the following day for Ithaca, with the same stalwart band of marines that supported us in Mycenae. It is a strange reversal of roles, that I am now on a mission to ask the king of Ithaca to come with me to Sparta; it does not seem very long ago that he was the one who called me to Troy.

It is a thoroughly pleasant voyage up the western shores of the Peloponnesus, past the islands of Zakynthos and Kefalonia to Ithaca. The prevailing wind in the Ionian Sea is known as the Maistro, and blows from the north-west, but rarely becomes as boisterous as the Etesians in the Aegean. The mild-mannered Maistro usually arrives in the early afternoon, delivers a reliable and steady breeze and dies down again in the evening.

We do not push the oarsmen because this voyage has none of the urgency of our return from Crete to Sparta, or our mission from Sparta to Mycenae. However, it is impossible for them not to give it everything they have, and in just over two days, our swift trireme is entering a sheltered bay, overlooked by verdant, mountainous country. Drawn up on the beach are ten biremes in various states of disrepair, while out in the bay we passed fifty or more fishing boats. On top of a tall hill, overlooking the sea, are the imposing towers of the palace of Odysseus. I do not doubt that the king is aware of our arrival.

Leaving the men to guard our ship, which is also well stocked with supplies for them, Pericles and I make our way up the hill towards the twin towers. We have come bearing gifts from King Menelaus, which wildly exceed anything in the usual Spartan tradition of austerity: a double-handled, gold drinking cup and gold pitcher, which I have never seen used at the palace.

At the top of the hill, the twin towers rear themselves a good sixty feet in the air. The massive gate between them is open, and a broad-shouldered figure in a purple cloak is striding towards us, unaccompanied. I was not expecting such a welcome. Pericles says, 'Does he never have a bodyguard?'

'He fears nothing and no one.'

We halt and bow deeply as the king approaches. He looks unchanged since he first arrived on Sparta's shores in the ship with the faded red sail: the dark eyes that quickly take everything in and give nothing away; the strong, wiry build of a soldier and an adventurer. He is smiling. 'How glad I am that I have regained Ithaca in time to welcome you!'

I am not sure that I have heard him correctly. 'You have been to another war, sir?'

He motions us to follow him into the palace. 'Only recently returned from Troy, master shipbuilder. On the voyage back, I was frequently detained by hosts who could not bear to part with their guest.'

He laughs at my horrified expression. 'Come, now! I have heard that it took you some time to be restored to your Spartan shipyard.' He gestures towards the bay. 'And I see that you have been extremely busy since you returned there. Ithaca would benefit from a few warships like that!'

As we enter the main hall, preparations are underway for a hearty meal: a pig is roasting on a spit in the fireplace; the smell of baking bread wafts in from the kitchens; and flagons of red wine are being set out on the table. A shaggy hound sleeps before the hearth. Pericles gracefully presents our gifts. 'Our king hopes soon to renew his friendship with you, sir.'

'The hope is mutual. And is it the case that "soon" could be imminent?'

He seats us with him at the table, calling for wine to be poured. And I tell him the whole horrible story of the vengeance that has been wreaked since Agamemnon arrived home from Troy to find death waiting for him. For several minutes after I finish, the king is silent, his dark eyes gazing reflectively into the fire that crackles and sizzles in the hearth. Then he murmurs, 'The act that was begun for the wrong reason and wilfully continued for the wrong reason has now gathered such momentum that it is going to be hard to stop.' He looks at Pericles. 'Did you know, as

Damian does, that Queen Helen was never at Troy during the entire war?'

The grotesqueness of this fact is such that I could never bring myself to share it with anyone. Looking stunned, Pericles shakes his head. 'No, sir.'

I say to the king, 'That is what this trial must do, sir. It must stop the machine of vengeance followed by more vengeance.'

'And Princess Electra wishes me to be her advocate. I wonder why that is.'

Pericles now answers. 'In my city of Athens, sir, they would have turned to the oracle; they do not do that in Sparta.'

The king looks at me. 'They do not normally use advocates in Sparta either; it is usually more of a court martial – is that correct, master shipbuilder?'

'That is correct, sir. The reason we felt that Electra and Orestes should each have an advocate is to try and be as fair as possible to both defendants. The trial must not just be fair – it must be seen to be fair.'

'That is commendable. But if you wish me to be Electra's advocate, you must share with me all the knowledge that you have.'

'Gladly, sir!'

Queen Penelope, Odysseus's graceful wife, joins us at supper. Smiling at me and Pericles, she says in mock-reproach, 'And are you two young adventurers about to steal my husband from me again for the foreseeable future?'

We both jump up and bow deeply; a smile lingers on the face of Odysseus, and I wonder at a marriage that has survived with such tenacity over so many years of absence. My face hot with embarrassment, I stammer, 'Gracious Majesty, we are only just now discovering how long it was before you were reunited with your lord. I can promise that this will be a short absence only and assure you of our gratitude to you in sparing the king.'

She smiles like sunshine blazing from behind a cloud. 'Oh, my good lord knows well that I can tolerate a few months when it was so many years! Now, be seated and tell me all about what is afoot in Sparta.'

King Odysseus adds, 'You also owe me an account of your time in Crete, master shipbuilder. I have heard that your life was saved by a most beautiful sea nymph there!'

Astonished at how quickly news travels across oceans, I recount what happened after my battered ship left Troy. When Pericles tells how the Athenians' story and that of Chrysothemis and me became one, King Odysseus is deeply interested. 'And now the labyrinth is very possibly completely underwater? You have all had a lucky escape!'

'But we hear that during your absence there was much treachery plotted here in Ithaca, sir.'

'And well those thieves have paid for it!' He recounts how the many suitors for the hand of his wife lived at his expense for years in his castle, even scheming to take the life of his son Telemachus, who made long journeys in the quest for information about his missing father.

King Odysseus gets up to place another log on the fire and stares into the flames. 'I consider that we were among the lucky ones. For too many, the legacy of Troy was betrayal and death. It is time that these Furies were contained.'

*

As we speed through the Ionian Sea the following morning, the steady Maistro winds now filling our sails, King Odysseus congratulates us heartily on our fast and powerful trireme; I decide to speak to King Menelaus about making the Ithacan king a gift of several warships, in gratitude for the service he is rendering to us.

King Menelaus has a warm welcome waiting for his old friend, and that evening a splendid banquet is held, which surpasses anything I have ever seen at the palace. Inevitably, the talk comes round to the trial, for which a date has now been set and a panel of Elders convened. King Odysseus remarks, 'I would like to visit Princess Electra tomorrow, to begin to prepare her advocacy.'

'That will be arranged,' replies Menelaus.

'In view of what we know about this young lady, it will also be necessary for there to be armed guards, as well as a witness and a scribe at my interviews.'

Looking ethereal in pale-blue silk, Chryso agrees. 'An essential precaution, sir.'

Odysseus looks at her with kindly eyes. 'You have suffered much at your sister's hands, my lady. I am glad for your sake that it is nearly over.'

'I am glad that you are here to help bring it to an end, sir.'

Odysseus turns to me. 'It would, I think, be very useful if you were my witness, master shipbuilder. In view of your role as advocate for Orestes, you will find it helpful too.'

'I will be honoured to serve, sir.'

Hermione joins the conversation. 'Damian, when you

interview Orestes, you will need a scribe and a witness too, surely?'

I look across at Odysseus and he nods, with a slight smile. I reply, 'If you are offering to be my witness, my lady, I accept with humble thanks.'

Her hazel eyes sparkle, and I think I know what Odysseus's smile meant: Hermione would like to spend more time in the company of her cousin. Recalling how Orestes looked at her when thanking her, I would be surprised if the feeling was not mutual.

*

When we enter Electra's cell the following day, she is handcuffed and tied to the chair where she is sitting. She is dressed in a plain prison robe, but she looks well groomed and self-possessed. The hair is pulled back severely from the square brow; the eyes are as hard and unblinking as ever. I imagine that she would disguise well as a man; there is little of the feminine about her. She stares at Odysseus and ignores everyone else. 'You find me at a disadvantage, sir. I cannot stand to greet you.'

He replies calmly, 'On the contrary, it is to your advantage that you are bound, my lady. It will prevent you from attempting something that you might regret.'

Already he has scored. Her ruse to get herself untied has been neatly turned on its head. We seat ourselves; the scribe prepares himself; and the interview begins. Throughout, Odysseus's tone is level, his delivery measured. I resolve to learn much from him.

'You have requested that I be your advocate in your forthcoming trial. Do you understand what an advocate can do and what he cannot?'

Her eyes narrow. 'Is this to be an interrogation?'

'You have not answered me, so I will provide the answer myself. If I am to speak on your behalf, what you tell me must be the truth; I can speak the truth on your behalf. What I cannot and will not do is lie for you. Do you understand that, my lady?'

Her voice is as distrustful as her eyes. 'What makes you think that I will lie to you?'

'I will ask the questions, my lady. If you do not answer them, this interview is at an end. I repeat, do you understand that you must tell me the truth?'

'Yes, yes, of course I understand! I'm not an idiot like my stupid brother!'

'Let us start with the day you abducted Princess Chrysothemis from the shores of Crete. Why did you do that?'

Electra laughs. 'Is that what she told you? It's a lie! She was eager to return to her home.'

'So eager that she had already refused to accompany her brother?'

'That moron? He couldn't pick his nose without help!'

'So eager, that it took two hundred fully armed warriors to force her into submission?'

'They were there to protect us from pirates. She came willingly on board.'

'When the alternative was that her lover would be cut to pieces by your soldiers, what would you expect her to do?'

She speaks as though I am not there. 'He has a grand view of himself if he thinks he is her lover. She will marry a prince of her own rank who will be chosen by me.'

'What did you intend to do with Princess Chrysothemis when she was back at Mycenae?'

'She would resume normal family life in the palace, of course.'

At that response, I have to look down at the floor to conceal my disgust. As if there had ever been anything normal about life or death in that accursed place.

'Do you know what her reasons were for running away to Crete some years before?'

'Some childish rebellion at having to grow up, I imagine.'

'You do not think it could have been grief at the sacrifice of her sister Iphigenia?'

'I showed my grief by going into mourning! That's what she should have done.'

'You do not think that it could have been fear of her mother's plans for killing King Agamemnon when he returned from the Trojan War, to avenge the sacrifice of their daughter Iphigenia?'

'Whatever my mother was planning to do was her business and no one else's.'

Odysseus pauses momentarily to allow the scribe to catch up. Then he says, 'Let us move on now to the banquet that was held on the night of the murders. If Princess Chrysothemis was to resume normal family life in the palace, why was she not at the banquet?'

There is the tiniest fraction of a pause, while Electra flicks a glance at me, realising that she cannot insist that

Chryso was at the banquet. 'She was feeling unwell. She was resting in her room.'

Odysseus's tone remains serenely level. 'She was in her room, tied to a chair, very much as you are now, my lady. Only she was also gagged, to prevent her from calling for help.'

'Whoever told you that is lying!'

'That night, you were planning to kill your mother and her lover Aegisthus, as revenge for their murder of your father. Is that correct?'

'It was Orestes' idea. He had been told by the oracle at Delphi that he must avenge his father.'

'What did you think of this idea, coming from the brother you call a moron?'

Another tiny hesitation, a flick of the hard eyes towards me and then back to Odysseus. 'The gods must be obeyed, even if we sometimes do not like their commands.'

'Even if their commands are to slit the throat of your own mother?'

'That is what Orestes believed, and that is what he did.'

'You are saying that it was Orestes who killed Queen Clytemnestra and Aegisthus, her paramour?'

'He was the one whom the gods had instructed.'

'He may have been instructed, but did he obey orders?'

She speaks woodenly now. 'He killed them.'

'This brother who – to quote you – cannot pick his nose without help, carried out a double murder that night?'

'He killed them.'

Odysseus waits until the scribe has finished writing, then he stands. 'I will leave you to reflect on why it was your clothes, not his, that were so covered in blood that you ordered your maidservant to burn them. Fortunately for us and unfortunately for you, she did not burn your dress; it is in our possession as evidence. You have three days to reflect, my lady. Use them well!'

*

The following day, Hermione, Odysseus and I ride out to the safe house, accompanied by the scribe in a small carriage. It is warm and sunny, so once more we sit in the garden. When Orestes joins us, it is clear that his health has continued to improve. With a new energy, he strides towards us, bows to Hermione – 'My lady, thank you for coming!' – and then bows deeply to Odysseus. 'Sir, it is a great honour to meet you; I have heard much about you.'

Odysseus smiles a slightly mischievous smile. 'Do not believe everything they tell you, Prince!'

As we seat ourselves, Orestes offers Hermione the chair next to his, which she is very happy to accept, smiling graciously at him. 'I would not want anyone else to be your witness, cousin – I am sure I shall excel at it!'

'I am sure you shall, my lady.' He has put on some muscle and his tanned skin tells of riding and walking in the sun. His eyes shine and he speaks with a confidence that makes Hermione's eyes sparkle again.

Odysseus kindly leads into the interview. 'I am here really as a mentor for Damian as he is new to this role. But I can assure you that you may all have every confidence in him, with his comprehensive knowledge of the background to this forthcoming trial. The role of the advocate is simply to speak truth for the defendant. Damian will do this well.'

What a contrast to that gloomy cell do we have in this bright garden, with its sun-dappled grass and birdsong from the fig trees. And as I think back to all the lies that were told in that prison, I now remember one lie that may have slipped through without King Odysseus noticing. The scribe is ready; Hermione cannot take her eyes off Orestes; and Odysseus is noting this with another discreet smile, as I begin: 'Brother, may I take you back to the time when you were a student studying in Athens. How did you find out that the oracle had told you to avenge your father?'

'Electra came to Athens; she was the one who told me. She had come to fetch me home.' I see Odysseus look towards the young man, as he picks up my drift.

'So, you did not go to consult the oracle?'

'And question my sister's judgement? She would have given me another of her tongue-lashings!'

'Was there confirmation from any other source that the gods wished you to kill your mother and her paramour?'

'Electra spoke as if it was common knowledge. It was many years since I had dared to argue with her about anything.'

'So, you only had her word for it?'

Orestes' handsome features darken as he frowns. 'I suppose I did. I never thought about it at the time.'

'How did you feel when she gave you this "news"?'

'Revulsion. I felt very ill.'

'You had no desire to obey the so-called "orders"?'

'I hoped that I might contract a serious illness and die before I had to do such a thing.' He speaks slowly and without emotion, almost as though he is talking about someone else. Hermione's eyes are full of unshed tears. I think she would like to lean forward and take his hand.

'This will be difficult for you, brother, but we now need to go to the night of the murders. You and Electra were dining in the banqueting hall, seated either side of your mother and her lover Aegisthus. And Princess Chrysothemis was a prisoner under guard in her bedroom.'

He swallows before replying quietly, 'Yes.'

'Do you know what Electra's intentions were with regard to her sister?'

He takes a quick breath. 'Electra had talked of "entertainment" before I was to kill our mother and Aegisthus.'

'And you knew what that meant?'

'She was planning to kill our sister herself. I think she had always hated her.'

'Why is that, do you think?'

'Because Chryso was everything she was not. Beautiful. Happy. Loving and loved.'

'How did she react when she realised that her sister had escaped?'

'At first, she thought I had released her. Then she realised that wasn't possible; she had never let me out of her sight. By now it was the early hours of the morning. She decided that it was time for me to… obey the orders… She thrust the knife into my hands.'

The birdsong has ceased. The garden is very quiet. Hermione clenches her fists as she sees Orestes relive that dreadful command. He stares at the ground, as though he sees Hades yawning in front of him. This is a dangerous moment. I reach across and grasp his hand. 'You are among friends, brother! There is no need for fear. Take your time.'

At that instant, Hermione reaches for his other hand with both of hers. 'You are among friends who love you dearly, cousin!' He looks up at her as though he has been dragged back from the edge of an abyss. Then, he says in a whisper, 'I told Electra that I could not do it. That I could never do it. Then, I waited for her to kill me.'

The silence in the garden reigns like a dark spell as I ask, 'What did she do?'

'She tore the knife from my hand and ran into our mother's bedroom.' Orestes is trembling violently. 'I am sorry. I can tell you no more.'

I wrap an arm around his shaking shoulders. 'We know from the evidence what happened next. The interview is over, brother.'

Hermione's hands are still firmly clasping that of Orestes; she is never going to let him go. King Odysseus remains looking thoughtfully at the young couple until the scribe has finished writing. Then, he says to Hermione, 'My lady, there is no reason now why your cousin should not be accommodated in the palace. I will speak with the king as soon as we get back. In the meantime, your cousin should not be alone; it would be wise for you to remain with him until we send a carriage for you both.'

ELEVEN
A HIGHER POWER

Three days after his first interview with Electra, King Odysseus goes again to see her with me and the scribe. The guards are present as before. This time Odysseus asks them to untie the ropes that bind Electra to the chair and the handcuffs that tie her wrists together. Rubbing her arms to restore the circulation, and flexing her legs with an exploratory prowl around the cell, Electra asks ironically, 'What is this, my lord Odysseus? Liberation?'

Seating himself, he replies calmly, 'Freedom to tell the truth, my lady. If you refuse, I will not lie for you. You will personally tell your lies to the Elders of the Spartan court.'

'I have told you nothing but the truth!'

'You lie. Try again, my lady.'

'I have been lied to!'

'Only by yourself. Again.'

'It was all my brother's doing! He was the one who killed them!'

Odysseus's voice never loses its calm. 'Disproved. Where will you run next, my lady?'

Freed from her bindings, Electra stalks the cell, looking from Odysseus to me to the scribe, then out of the barred window. Despite the guards, she terrifies me. Suddenly, she turns from the window and draws herself up to her full height. Anticipating an assault, both guards warningly draw their swords. But she does not move, saying with the authority of a high priestess, 'I did kill them! But I was right to do so – the gods commanded it!'

'In what way did the gods command it?'

'The oracle told Orestes that he must avenge his father.'

'No, my lady. You told him.'

She hisses, 'You are no stranger to deception! I have heard that you pretended to be mad rather than go to Troy!'

'I am not about to go on trial for it. So, you admit that you lied to your brother about the oracle.' He glances at the scribe, who is busy taking it all down.

'It was *true* that my father's murder had to be avenged.'

'Even though it was he who brought about the death of your sister Iphigenia, for whom you are still in mourning?'

'He too was obeying the gods.'

King Odysseus now stands. Although he is no taller than she is, the intensity of the gaze from his dark eyes causes her to look away. 'Let us be absolutely clear about what you want me to say on your behalf to this court. That you confess to murdering Queen Clytemnestra and Aegisthus but that the killings were justified because they were ordered by the gods.'

And now a change comes over Electra's pale, angular face. 'No. I do not wish you to say anything on my behalf. You will twist everything to make me look guilty, when I am thoroughly vindicated. I will conduct my own defence!'

*

Odysseus and I go to the shipyard after the final interview with Electra. I had spoken to Menelaus, and he eagerly grasped the opportunity to make a gift to his friend that would be greatly valued. He has offered to have ten triremes built especially for Ithaca. So, we now go to see Paros to discuss the designs for the royal livery that these ships will bear and any special emblems that are dear to the heart of the king. I have never seen Odysseus so animated. 'On all ten of the warships, I would like a symbol for the Maistro wind that finally carried me home. On the first three to be built, I would like each ship to be named: Penelope, for my beautiful and long-suffering wife; Telemachus for my faithful and stalwart son; and Eumaeus, for the loyal swineherd who did not even recognise me when I returned but still obeyed the ancient laws of hospitality. These precious three I treasure the chance to honour!'

Moved by the king's great joy at coming home, and remembering how I felt on my return to Sparta, I have an idea. We three are looking out over the shipyard and the harbour, when I say, 'Why do we not commemorate these new bonds between our two countries with an annual ship race? One year, Ithaca to Sparta and back; the next, vice versa?'

King Odysseus mightily likes this, and Paros can see the advantages of our two countries remaining firm allies. 'Let us put it to King Menelaus tonight.' We are all dining at the palace this evening; the trial is in three days' time.

*

The following morning, I am working in the shipyard on the first of Odysseus's ships when Paros calls across to me and points to the far horizon. The insect-like silhouettes of a vast flotilla are advancing towards our shores. Paros says, 'My money is on Pyrrhos. We need to nip this in the bud, Vice-Admiral! I will go to the barracks and muster troops.'

'And I will fetch King Odysseus.' I set off at a run for the palace.

By the time the Myrmidons beach, they are met by a phalanx of bronze-armoured soldiers with interlocked shields, spears levelled directly at them; at their head is King Odysseus, fully armed and armoured. Pyrrhos has lost none of the swagger he displayed on his first visit; he must consider that, with 2,500 warriors behind him, he has no need to kneel to anyone. Unsheathing his sword, he approaches Odysseus. In perfect synchrony, without any orders needed, the Spartan troops take a single step forwards to stand close behind the king. It is Odysseus who utters the first words: 'We in Sparta are being very generous, Prince, although your behaviour does not deserve it! You have one chance to keep your freedom and one only: you must depart these shores now and never return. If you fail to obey us, you will be arrested and tried for triple murder.'

Taken aback, but unused to obeying orders of any kind, Pyrrhos growls: 'I am come to claim Hermione, daughter of Menelaus, as my bride. You will not turn me back from that!' With the lightning speed and purpose for which Spartans are famous, four soldiers seize Pyrrhos, disarm him and bind him. Before he can utter a word, he is dragged away to be thrown in prison.

With their leader suddenly gone, the Myrmidons are in complete disarray. One step after another, the Spartans advance on them, a wall of spears and shields. A few of Pyrrhos's men throw their spears; they bounce off Spartan armour and rattle to the ground. Odysseus now raises his voice so that the command booms across the bay. 'Begone Myrmidons and be quick about it, or we will hound you in our warships to the ends of the ocean!' The Spartans' relentless advance continues as the Myrmidons break ranks and scramble for their ships. Again, with no orders needed, the Spartan line halts; motionless, the troops watch the Myrmidons' biremes pull away from our beaches.

Odysseus turns to me with a grim smile. 'That was a very effective strategy, Vice-Admiral.'

'It took you to command it, sir.'

'The son of Achilles has acted towards us as an enemy would. He has forfeited any right to leniency.'

'And he will now stand in the same court as Electra, to be called to account for acts, not of war, but of murder.'

Odysseus's dark eyes look at me closely. 'Were you not tempted to arraign him on his first visit here?'

‘He came as a potential ally; although, it would have been a dangerous allegiance if he had discovered that Orestes was here.’

‘And his ships never did carry out a blockade of Knossos harbour as had been agreed?’

‘In the event it was not necessary. But it showed us that Pyrrhos always has an agenda of his own, even if it is not of his own choosing.’

‘He feels utterly bound to avenge his father…’

‘Yes, and that is why I felt sorry for him at first; he seemed as much a victim of the gods as Orestes. But now I think that he would happily commit those murders all over again.’

And now, King Odysseus says something that I was not expecting at all. ‘If I were not to be called as the chief witness against Pyrrhos, I would offer to be his advocate. Had you considered offering to speak for him? You two had a kind of camaraderie at Troy, after all.’

His words make me stop and think, remembering our wordless friendship. We have both lost our fathers. Pyrrhos is very alone. I wonder if he would accept. I wonder also if I am capable of putting the right words together. I am not at all sure that I am.

*

Like a true Spartan, King Menelaus does not show that he is angry at Pyrrhos’s actions, but his mouth tightens, and his blue eyes have a cold light. ‘So, his old deeds will return to accuse him in the courtroom,’ he murmurs. ‘It is fitting that two who murdered in the name of the gods will now face Spartan justice!'

When King Odysseus and I go to see him in his cell, Pyrrhos is like a fire mountain that is ready to explode. With his colossal strength and anger, he has to be contained in a separate chamber from us, where he is chained to the wall. Again, I feel a pang of pity for this child who has never had the chance to grow up and understand what he must leave behind of his past. I think that Odysseus realises this too, because his tone is very gentle. 'Prince, you have to stand in court accused of slaying King Priam of Troy, his grandson Astyanax and his daughter Princess Polyxena. What do you have to say?'

In reply, Pyrrhos pounds the wall behind him with his chained hands until the blood runs. 'These were acts of war! When you sack a city, you do not leave anyone living who might retaliate! Any fool knows that!'

'How was the aged King Priam to come against you? How was his grandchild, little Astyanax, to attack you? How was Polyxena to retaliate?'

'The threat has to be eliminated! Self-serving factions can rise up in support of survivors! You yourself know that, King Odysseus!'

Odysseus asks, 'Were you pursuing vengeance for the death of your mighty father?'

'And always will. It was Apollo who guided the treacherous arrow of Paris; the idiot could never have had the skill to fire it himself.'

'Do you regret killing King Priam, the baby Astyanax and urging the sacrifice of Princess Polyxena?'

'I serve the gods of war and of vengeance, King Odysseus. And one day, I will go to the oracle and demand that Apollo pays reparation for the death of my father!'

Here, I think, could be a good time. 'Pyrrhos, will you let me speak for you? As your advocate, I think I could make a case for you.' I can hardly believe that I am saying this.

He stares at me as though noticing me for the first time in this meeting. 'What can you say that I cannot say for myself?'

'It's not so much what you say, it's how you say it. I can take the rage out of your words and put them to what is, in effect, a military court. Your argument needs to be put forward primarily as a military one.'

'You would take the gods out of it?'

'This is Sparta, Pyrrhos. Practically every man here is in the army or the navy.'

The powerful fists that have been clutching the chains that bind him relax slightly. 'Can I trust you, shipbuilder?'

'I have been your friend on occasions when many were not.'

'That is true. Then be my advocate, shipbuilder. I know that fancy words are not my strong point.'

'I will do my very best for you, my friend.' Coming into his cell, I offer my hand, knowing that he could break every bone in my body. He takes it firmly, his mouth tightening in that Pyrrhos approximation to a smile.

As we emerge from the cells, I say to Odysseus, 'If Pyrrhos is found guilty of the murders, what kind of penalty will the Spartan court impose?'

'What will they impose if Electra is found guilty? You

may know the answers to these questions better than I do, master shipbuilder. It is a military issue, is it not?'

'I know that in Sparta, to kill for any reason other than the defence of your country is the crime of murder. And I once heard of a general being executed for betraying a comrade to his death.'

'Do you think that the death penalty may not be appropriate in these cases?'

'Surely, if the murderer showed signs of remorse, there could be a case for reducing the sentencing to a jail term. And maybe, if any kind of reparation were possible…'

'Did you see any sign of remorse in Electra or Pyrrhos?'

'I wish I had.'

'And what kind of reparation could be made?'

'There you have me again, sir.'

'And do you think, once released from prison, either of these two might kill again?'

'Sir, you have put me in an impossible place. I think that either of them could kill again. They both seem so… careless about human life.'

'Then it would have to be imprisonment for life, would it not? The only other alternative is exile: Sparta has done that with unwanted foreigners, but not, as far as I know, with convicted murderers. However, there is a first time for everything.'

*

The trials begin the next day. They are held in the stadium normally used for chariot racing, in order to accommodate as many members of the public as possible. Security is tight, with troops patrolling in the stadium and in the streets. In the centre of the arena's sandy floor is a long table, around which are seated the Elders of the city who will judge this case. Opposite them is the dock where the defendant will be held under guard. To one side of the judges are the advocates, among whom I am seated, and the witnesses. Chryso, Hermione and King Menelaus are on the other side of the judges. Electra, Orestes and Pyrrhos are being held in separate cells until it is their turn to appear. King Menelaus has instructed the Elders to call Orestes first. A trumpet blast silences the buzzing audience, and the proceedings begin.

Orestes is brought to the dock under guard, and I am called as his advocate. My eyes fix his as I cross the arena to stand beside him. He looks calm and self-possessed. Hermione and Chryso are watching him intently.

I bow to the Elders. 'Sirs, it is my honour to speak for Prince Orestes in his defence: he is charged with murdering Queen Clytemnestra and her paramour Aegisthus. On the night that they died, the Princess Electra instructed Prince Orestes to kill the pair as they slept. She gave him a knife. He refused to carry out the act. She has confessed to taking the knife and stabbing them to death. This confession has been recorded and you have it in your possession. There is also evidence of Princess Electra's guilt and that, too, is in your possession. I proclaim my client to be entirely innocent and request that he walks from this court a free man.'

An excited murmur starts up in the assembled crowds and is instantly silenced by another trumpet blast. The

Elder in the centre of the table, who wears a purple robe that distinguishes him from the Spartan crimson of the others, rises to his feet. 'We do indeed have the confession, Master Advocate, and we have the evidence. It is now our duty to instruct His Highness Prince Orestes to walk free from the place where he stood accused.'

The guards open the gate of the box and there is a gasp, because they actually stand to attention and salute Orestes as he walks out of the dock and to me. The gasp becomes a gale of cheers and applause, as we walk together to take our seats next to King Menelaus and the princesses. Hermione's eyes are as bright as stars; I think they are full of tears of joy. King Menelaus stands and embraces his future son-in-law.

A hush descends as Electra is led into the arena. She stares straight ahead of her, as though she is walking in a different world. Once in the dock, her eyes look to the ground, taking no notice of anyone. King Odysseus is called as her advocate; he comes and bows before the panel of Elders and says, 'Honourable gentlemen, my client, Princess Electra, has decided that she will conduct her own defence without the assistance of an advocate.'

The Elder in the purple robe nods an acknowledgement. 'Thank you, Your Majesty. The panel will therefore interrogate her directly.'

As King Odysseus returns to his advocate's seat, the purple-robed Elder becomes in effect a prosecutor. 'The defendant will understand that she must answer every question that is put to her. Do you understand that, my lady Electra?'

She gives the briefest of nods.

'I repeat, you will answer every question that is put to you. A nod is not an answer!'

She mutters something that could be a yes.

'My lady, you do yourself no favours if your answers cannot be heard!'

Sullenly, she says, slightly more loudly, 'Yes.'

'You are charged with murdering Queen Clytemnestra and her paramour Aegisthus while they slept, following a banquet at the palace of Mycenae. You have confessed to the killings. Do you have anything to add to your confession?'

At this point, Electra raises her head and looks around the arena for the first time. Then she replies clearly and loudly, 'Yes, I do have something to add. The killings were lawful because they were commanded by Apollo!'

This sends the arena into uproar. Spartans are used to military courts, where witnesses are called, evidence is presented and evaluated, arguments for and against put forward, verdicts reached and sentences handed out accordingly. They have never before heard the gods invoked. Electra looks pleased at the reaction her shock statement has provoked. But then, the laughter begins. Electra had thought that Spartans must obviously take the gods as seriously as Mycenae and Athens do. She has made a terrible mistake. Her defence is, literally, being laughed out of court. Then begins the shouting. 'Matricide! Matricide!' Spartans' regard for the female sex is considerably greater than their respect for the gods.

It takes several trumpet blasts and a patrolling army cohort in the arena to bring the crowd to order. Finally, a near-silence descends and the chief Elder addresses Electra once more. His voice is measured and calm. 'My lady, if you think that the gods are to be regarded as a higher power than the cause of justice, then you are gravely mistaken. You have spoken and we have listened. Sentencing will follow our final case to be heard in this court.'

In a daze, barely able to believe what she has heard, Electra is led away. Chryso buries her face in her hands and sobs with relief. I hold her tightly, for a long time. It is almost over. Then I go to take my place with the advocates, as Pyrrhos is called and marched in, surrounded by a cohort of ten guards. Odysseus goes to stand with the witnesses.

The crowd is now very quiet; there is great interest in the valiant son of Achilles. Pyrrhos seems to sense that he may have more friends here than he thought. I persuaded the prison authorities to allow him to dress in his uniform and he cuts a fine figure in it.

Once more, I bow to the panel of Elders. 'Sirs, I am honoured to speak for Prince Pyrrhos, son of Achilles, and a distinguished and mighty warrior. He performed many acts of great bravery during the Troy wars but now stands accused of the murders of King Priam and Priam's grandson Astyanax, and the death by sacrifice of Princess Polyxena. He does not deny that he is responsible for the killings of these defenceless civilians. He simply hopes that you will hear him out on how the ways of war make very different demands to those of ordinary life. In listening to me, you are listening to Prince Pyrrhos.'

The chief Elder remains seated and says, 'Pray proceed, Master Advocate.'

I take a deep breath. 'Our fighting men are asked to give their all to protect their country. They make great sacrifices in that cause. They lose their comrades, their limbs and their lives. The battlefield, therefore, with its smoke and dust and heat and blood, is an entirely different world to the one that we normal mortals inhabit. It is one where the ethic is to survive to fight another battle, another day, in the defence of one's country. In that fight, the cost of failure can mean the end of all things. To ensure success, nothing can be left to chance. In pursuing military success, measures need to be taken which will horrify us ordinary mortals. Such were the deaths of which Prince Pyrrhos stands accused; they do horrify. But that is war; we cannot always take prisoners. Finally, I would remind this court that in Sparta, killing doing one's duty in the defence of one's country is not classed as murder. It is what it is to be a soldier.' I bow again to the Elders. 'Sirs, I thank you and this court for your courtesy in hearing me out.'

In the silence after I finish speaking, you could hear a feather fall. Glancing at Pyrrhos, I see his head humbly bowed; there are tears on his cheeks, as there were when we approached that Troy shore where his father and my father died.

The chief Elder stands. 'Master Advocate, we thank you for your words. They have given us much on which to dwell. There is no need to call any witnesses. This court will reconvene at the same time tomorrow for sentencing.' The trumpet blasts; the prisoner is marched off to his cell; and the crowds file out of the arena in almost total silence.

That evening, I go to visit Pyrrhos. Because of his calmer behaviour, he has been given a cell where he is not chained and where there is water and bread on a small table. As I enter, he is sleeping on his mattress like an exhausted child. He sleeps as one who has not slept for many days and nights. Again, I feel a stab of pity for him. If he had not been born the son of Achilles, what would his life be now? He might be married, a father with a wife to love and children to be proud of. I take a seat and watch him sleep.

When he stirs and his eyes finally open, he does not seem surprised to see me. He gets up and takes the chair opposite mine. 'You spoke well, shipbuilder.'

'They were words that needed to be said.'

'Will they execute me? I don't care if they do.'

'I don't see how they can, under the military law of Sparta.'

'Lock me away?'

'For you, that would be far worse than execution, wouldn't it?'

'If I could not escape, yes.'

'They could decide on exile. If they do, where would you go?'

'Delphi. Apollo has to atone for murdering my father.'

'How will you make him do that?'

'I will sack his temple if I have to!'

'Could you not take your exile as a second chance? Return to inherit your father's kingdom and take a wife?'

'My father should be alive now! Apollo must bring him back to me!'

This cry of utter heartbreak is still ringing in my ears as I take my place in the arena the next day. The two prisoners, Electra and Pyrrhos, stand with their guards: Electra, pale-faced and stony as ever; Pyrrhos, his copper hair blazing, radiating the energy of rage.

The kings Menelaus and Odysseus stand together, each in royal purple to mark the solemnity of the occasion. Orestes stands with Hermione, and Chryso, next to me, slips her hand into mine. The senior Elder stands, and silence reigns in the arena. 'We find that the Princess Electra bears considerably more guilt as a murderer than does Prince Pyrrhos, because of the carefully premeditated nature of her crime. The fact that Prince Pyrrhos was acting under the orders of war do not make the deaths for which he is responsible any less horrific, but that same fact is a mitigating element in the burden of guilt that he bears. The prince is therefore sentenced to permanent exile from these shores. The princess, we feel, will always represent a threat to the lives of others; she will therefore be incarcerated for the remainder of her life. Whether or not she can receive visitors will depend entirely on her conduct and her demonstration of remorse at her crimes.'

I look at Chryso; tears are running down her face. She weeps for both of her sisters, the victim and the destroyer. While the memory of that cry, the loneliness of the forsaken child Pyrrhos, will live with me always.

*

King Odysseus stayed with us for two more weeks so that he could attend a double wedding; low-key in true Spartan style, in the simple food and well-watered wine, but not in the number of guests. Chryso and Hermione decided to invite Sparta's entire navy and every shipyard worker, along with their families. And so, we used the chariot racing arena once more. With flowers raining down on us to the hearty cheers from all those men of the sea, it was a stirring event that was fondly remembered for years afterwards. And it was the powerful marine associations of that wedding which, I think, caused Chryso to form her plan, aided and abetted by Pericles and Athena.

We were walking along the beach by the shipyards, and Pericles was with us, accompanied by Melitta, who was holding the hand of Pericles' one-year-old son, Cimon, and encouraging his toddling steps. In the tender care of Pericles and Athena, Melitta had been able to leave behind her terrible past and step into the new world of a mother and father who loved her; with a baby brother to cuddle and adore.

While Melitta slows her pace to help little Cimon on his wobbly legs, Pericles and I are observing how quickly Odysseus's new fleet of triremes is being built and congratulating ourselves on the new, high-speed production systems. Then Chryso says to Pericles, 'Do you know how many other Athenian families are still living in Crete?'

He frowns. 'In the years before we had to go there, it could have been a great many.'

'And are they living mainly in the mountain villages, now they have left the labyrinth?'

'If you mean, would they have escaped the second wave, I can only hope that the answer is yes.'

'Do you think they are happy there?'

'I don't know how the local communities would have accepted them. Or how much the second wave might have damaged the crops of olive and fig trees. When times become hard, local people can turn against strangers in their midst.'

Chryso looks at me. 'I think we should go back and see what has happened. Perhaps we can help.'

King Menelaus is in agreement but advises a more cautious approach. 'I will instruct the Krypteia to carry out a reconnoitring mission first. Remember, Crete now has a navy again, thanks to Sparta – she may not welcome an incursion. But it would be very useful to have an assessment of her current naval strength.'

In just twelve days, a young Krypteian officer is bowing to us in the palace throne room. King Menelaus leads. 'Did you have the opportunity to make a tally of the number of warships?'

'We counted sixty-four, sir.'

'We gave them one hundred or so Mycenaean ships – does that mean that some were not in port?'

'The ships that we observed were not in a good state of repair, sir. This could be because they were on the water, rather than being housed in sheds on the dockside. We saw no sheds, sir.'

I look at the king. 'It would seem to indicate a lack of manpower to build the sheds, sir. As a formerly great naval power, Crete would know as well as anyone how to maintain her fleet.'

He nods. 'A combination of her shrinking population and the loss of life to the second wave, no doubt. Maybe Crete's glory days are over.'

Pericles says eagerly to the young officer, 'Did your

investigations reveal the extent of the Athenian population in Crete?'

'We found eleven families, sir. Their children had been forced into labour in Crete's shipyards – girls as well as boys. All were very poor.'

'How did their situation seem to compare with the rest of the population?'

'The Athenian families were living in huts near the shipyard, sir. While the native Cretans were fairly prosperous farmers, living in villages on the lower mountain slopes. They cultivate fig and olive trees and run goats and sheep.'

King Menelaus comments, 'So the Athenians may have helped to increase Crete's population, but they are not being treated as part of it?'

'They are little better than slaves, sir. And they are far more at risk than the native Cretans from another danger, as well.'

'What danger is that?'

'As we left to return to Sparta, we saw a thick column of black smoke issuing from the remains of the fire mountain, sir. There were flames within the smoke. There was also a pronounced roaring from beneath the sea.'

Chryso says quickly, 'Don't you see what this means? If the Athenians are forced to live near the dockside, then many must have been already lost to the first and second waves! And now it's going to happen all over again!'

*

Once more, we were in a race against time. King Menelaus sent a second force of Krypteians immediately to Crete, to warn the dockside families to prepare in secrecy for a total evacuation. Three triremes were stocked with provisions and manned with our finest oarsmen, including Pericles' men. Chryso and Athena were to be part of the expedition, as so many of our passengers would be women and children. King Menelaus came to the harbour to wish us a safe voyage. And it is not long before we are rowing flat out past the shores of Kythira, the powerful Etesians filling our sails. From the trireme he is captaining, Pericles gives me another of his cheerful waves.

We don't beat our twenty-two-hour record from Crete to Sparta, because we are heavily loaded with provisions, but twenty-four hours later, having rowed through the night, we are entering Knossos port. We have little fear of Knossos turning out in force to defend itself against the three Spartan triremes, each with their 170 armed marines, because the Cretans must be well aware of a far greater force that is threatening them. The dawn is obscured by colossal black clouds coiling skywards from the remains of the fire mountain. The roaring from the seabed is causing the water outside the harbour to boil and churn.

Shivering in the chill air, clutching their few possessions, a ragged crowd of maybe forty men, women and children waits on the quayside, five Krypteian officers in calm attendance. As we hasten their boarding, my greatest fear is that, suddenly, this restless water will disappear, sucked out towards the horizon, and leave our ships helplessly grounded, with no choice but to await the third giant wave that will sweep us all to certain death. As the minutes creep by, it is easy to imagine, with every swirl of the tide, that the water is already in retreat.

All are aboard; the Krypteia are returning to their ship; and our oarsmen are straining every muscle to get us out of this doomed harbour. It is now as dark as night. Wide-eyed and terrified, the Athenian children huddle beneath the bulkheads, while Chryso and Athena comfort the fearful mothers. As we leave the harbour and enter the open sea, our triremes and our oarsmen are now tested to their very limit by waves that tower over us. They are so huge that we climb up one side like a mountain, teeter for a second at the crest, then pitch downwards into the trough. On the crest, intense upwards pressure is being applied to the centre of the hull; then we hit the trough like a wall of stone, testing the ship's impact absorption to the extreme. But Paros will be proud of me – the mighty twin cables do their job, and our ships hold firm in this apocalyptic sea.

By the time we pass Antikythira, the wind has blown away the dark clouds from the fire mountain; the morning sun is shining on us; and the wave height is much decreased. Honey bread and water are passed round our passengers, and the oarsmen work in shifts so that everyone has a chance to fill their bellies. All through the afternoon, schools of dolphins escort us on our voyage towards Kythira, causing the children to shout with delight. This time, it is Chryso who remembers the dolphin fresco in the labyrinth. 'They were so lifelike and so joyous – just like these! Maybe we have more in common than we think with those wonderful beings from so long ago.'

I reach out a hand and gently touch her cheek. 'Maybe we do.'

Night has fallen by the time we begin the final leg to Sparta's shores. As we enter the harbour, traces of a rosy dawn are trailing in the east. And I am greatly moved to see King Menelaus, Hermione and Orestes together with a cohort of soldiers lining the harbour side, lighting our way to the beach with flaming torches. Temporary accommodation has been arranged in the homes of the citizens of Sparta, and they are waiting to collect their guests and put a roof over their heads.

When all have departed, and the triremes moved safely back into their housings by the crews, Chryso and I follow the king back to the palace, where we now have an apartment of our own. One thought, a regret, has been overshadowing my mind ever since Chryso pointed out the massive urgency of the rescue. 'I wish we could have helped all the Athenians to escape when we took the couples from the labyrinth. I feel that we have failed those who perished in the first and second waves.'

Chryso slips her arm through mine, in the lovely way that she has taken to since we became man and wife. She says softly, 'We have snatched them all from the waves, merman. I was talking to one of the wives on the way back. She told me that the Athenians were only made to work in the Knossos shipyards after the second wave; before that, they were slaves working on farms in the mountain villages. So, we grieve for the tragedy of the poor Cretans who died, but we rejoice in saving all of Pericles' kinsmen.'

The Krypteian unit that organised the evacuation made landfall twelve hours after us. They had stayed on the sheltered west shore of the island to observe for as long as it was safe to do so. Finally judging it wise to beat a retreat, they put a good distance between themselves and the island and, turning, saw a wave so vast that it seemed to draw the very clouds with it as it hurtled towards Knossos.

*

Two months later, Pericles is our leader, as we deliver the ten magnificent triremes to the verdant island of Ithaca. He has promised to train the crews of King Odysseus in the complex art of rowing the three banks of oars. As we approach the shore, we can see the ten new housings on the sloping beach, where the timbers of the stout hulls will be protected from the elements. Odysseus and his queen smilingly greet our arrival, while a small army of trainee mariners look on with shining eyes at their new warships. Pericles is captaining Queen Penelope's ship, and he has it drawn up onto the beach so that she can admire the artwork. 'Why,' she smiles, 'who is this sea nymph gracing the prow of my ship?'

I see Odysseus for the first time ever momentarily at a loss for words and remember his teasing comment on the sea nymph who saved my life on the island of Crete. Finding it hard not to smile, I recall that the artist would have had no idea what Penelope looked like, beautiful though she is. But he would have had a ready reference in the golden-haired, blue-eyed princess who, with her cousin, visited Sparta's shipyards so regularly. It really is quite amusing to see the clever king of Ithaca caught out by his wife. Chryso found it equally funny to be pictured on the prow of a king's flagship. Although, I think it would be better if she and Queen Penelope never meet. The king's wife tolerated his long and wandering journey home after Troy with admirable fortitude, but I doubt if she would want to know too much detail about his encounters with sea nymphs.

On the final night of our stay on Ithaca, once all his crews are expert in getting the new triremes to skim across the bay and fly ahead of the Maistro wind, Odysseus throws a splendid banquet. But before we begin, his face is grave. 'I am very sorry to tell you that I have heard today of the death of Pyrrhos, son of Achilles. After he was sent into exile, he did not return to the kingdom he would have inherited. I wish he could have put aside the anger he felt against Apollo for killing his father; but it was as self-destructive as the rage that Achilles himself felt when he quarrelled with Agamemnon over Briseis. Instead, Pyrrhos went to the sanctuary of Apollo, the Olympian god of light, knowledge and harmony: an immortal who, we know, is not averse to killing mortals. It is not clear what Pyrrhos thought he could achieve. Some say he went to plunder Apollo's temple; others that he demanded that Apollo atone for the murder of Achilles.' King Odysseus stares into the fire, his dark eyes reflecting the flames. 'It would appear that the priests of Apollo set upon the son of Achilles and killed him. Knowing what we do about Pyrrhos's mighty strength as a warrior, I would say that he chose not to defend himself but went willingly to the slaughter. Perhaps it was the only route he could see to being reunited with his beloved father. Let us raise a cup to his memory.'

*

On the way back to Sparta, I take an oar with Pericles on his ship. The Maistro is blowing strongly from the north-west and we are making good speed across the waves. But it can never be fast enough for me; I am desperate to get home and hold Chryso in my arms. From somewhere back on that distant Troy shore come the howls of the Furies mingled with the murmur of the steady wind that powers us on.

As though he can read my thoughts, Pericles says quietly, 'We were prisoners in the labyrinth while Greeks and Trojans were dying.'

'I built the horse that killed babies, young girls and old men.'

'You also built the ships that saved us all from a terrible death. Let that be enough, brother.'

*

Once again, I am drawing in the sand, as I show Pericles the new design of mainsail that is my current obsession. In the harbour, the sail of *Flying Fish* is catching the breeze, skilfully set by Pericles' four-year-old son, Cimon, with my two-year-old Stergios his attentive crew. As well as showing all the signs of promising mariners, both are learning fast how to build ships. On the harbour side, Pericles' wife Athena and my Chrysothemis call encouragingly to helm and crew. Straightening up, I take a step back and survey my work. And, as a matter of habit, cast a quick glance behind me at the horizon. The Aegean serenely reflects a cloudless blue sky, completely empty of sails and any other presence, human or divine. I turn back to Pericles. He nods his approval of my sail and together we walk into the waves to join our children.